SANTA'S NAUGHTY HELPER

A BAD BOY CHRISTMAS ROMANCE

MICHELLE LOVE

CONTENTS

About the Author	vii
Sign Up to Receive Free Books	ix
Blurb	xi
1. Clay	1
2. Alexis	6
3. Clay	11
4. Alexis	16
5. Clay	20
6. Alexis	24
7. Clay	29
8. Alexis	34
9. Clay	39
10. Alexis	43
11. Clay	48
12. Alexis	53
13. Clay	58
14. Alexis	63
15. Clay	67
16. Alexis	71
17. Clay	75
18. Alexis	79
19. Clay	85
20. Alexis	89
Sign Up to Receive Free Books	93
Preview of Her Dark Secret	95
Chapter One	97
Chapter Two	101
Chapter Three	109
Chapter Four	125
Chapter Five	131
Other Books By This Author	134
About the Author	137

Copyright 138

Made in "The United States" by:

Michelle Love

© Copyright 2020 – Michelle Love

ISBN: 978-1-64808-139-2

ALL RIGHTS RESERVED. No part of this publication may be reproduced or transmitted in any form whatsoever, electronic, or mechanical, including photocopying, recording, or by any informational storage or retrieval system without express written, dated and signed permission from the author

❀ Created with Vellum

ABOUT THE AUTHOR

Mrs. Love writes about smart, sexy women and the hot alpha billionaires who love them. She has found her own happily ever after with her dream husband and adorable 6 and 2 year old kids.

Currently, Michelle is hard at work on the next book in the series, and trying to stay off the Internet.

"Thank you for supporting an indie author. Anything you can do, whether it be writing a review, or even simply telling a fellow reader that you enjoyed this. Thanks

 facebook.com/HotAndSteamyRomance
 instagram.com/michellesromance

SIGN UP TO RECEIVE FREE BOOKS

Sign Up to Receive Free E-Books and Audiobook Codes.

Would you like to read **The Unexpected Nanny, Dirty Little Virgin** and **other romance books** for free?

You can sign up to receive these free e-books and audiobooks by typing this link into your browser:

https://www.steamyromance.info/free-books-and-audiobooks-hot-and-steamy/

Or this one:

https://www.steamyromance.info/the-unexpected-nanny-free/

BLURB

Clay Jordan

**I'm the type of guy you don't tell what to do.
I'm the guy who knows what he wants. I bend the rules: things go my way, and I don't pay the consequences.**
So, when I get into legal and financial trouble, I'm more than happy to take the plea deal to avoid a scandal.
And what is that deal? Playing the part of Santa in one of the largest malls in New York.
I'll get through it, go through the motions.
Then I meet Alexis.
She's timid, she's innocent, she's sexy.
She should be on the Nice List for sure, but I'll put her on the Naughty List.

Alexis Simone:

School has been hectic, and I'm learning charities are impossible to start.

Either way, I'm determined. My twin sister passed away from leukemia when we were kids, and I've made it my life's goal to find the cure.

I'm not alone, but then, I am.
I throw myself into charities. I'm not afraid of hard work, and not interested in getting involved with the hotshots who show up to these events to pick up chicks.
Although I wasn't planning on meeting Clay.
He's young, he's rich, and he's just the guy I'll never love.
But when he looks at me, my knees buckle. I'm putty in his hands.
And he knows it.

It's the holiday season in the Big Apple, and the spirit of Christmas is in the air. At least, it is for the rest of the city. Clay Jordan has recently found himself in the middle of a legal battle, and he's not sure how he'll get out of it without making headlines once again.
When he's given the option of volunteering for charity over jailtime, he takes it in a heartbeat, but he's far from happy about it. Until he meets Alexis. She's young, beautiful, driven, and most of all, innocent. She's not at all his type, but is the exact woman that he needs. He's got her in his sights, but it's clear she's not interested.
Or is she?
Subtle hints, and a hot moment under the mistletoe, are what it takes to break the ice between them, and soon Alexis finds herself head over heels for a man she knows is a bad scheme. Except, for the first time in her life, she's ready to be naughty.

1

CLAY

"Bottom line, Larry, how bad is it?" I ask impatiently. "Stop giving me the runaround and tell it to me straight."

There's a pause on the other end of the line followed by a sigh. "It's not good, Clay, that's how it is. You know the IRS frowns upon tax evasion. How do you think so many CEOs end up in prison?" He laughs, but I don't join in. I'm guilty, and don't want this to blow up into yet another scandal.

In the past few years, my name has been in the headlines more than once. From hooking up with the wrong women to getting involved in the wrong foreign trades, it seems I can't stay out of the public's eye. Not that I care what they think. I have more money than I know what to do with, and so far it hasn't held me back in my ambitions.

Even the bigger issues I've faced haven't stopped me from getting new business partners, investors, and people asking me to invest with them. I can have any woman I want, anytime I want, discard her in the morning, and move onto the next.

Honestly, I've been on top of my game throughout my twenties and well into my thirties, becoming one of the youngest self-made billionaires in history.

"I'm not seeing what's funny about this," I say dryly. The laughter stops, and he clears his throat.

"No, there is nothing funny about this at all," he says. "But it also doesn't make sense to stress out about something you cannot control."

"You are the one with control over this!" I snap. "They said you were the best lawyer in New York City! I'm depending on you to get this entire thing swept under the rug and kept out of the papers!"

"That is the ultimate goal here. I know you're stressed about this, but don't be! There's a reason they call me the best. If you can just settle down, all of this will go a lot smoother," Larry replies condescendingly, and if he were in the room, I'd likely punch him.

I hate working with lawyers. They are all the same. More focused on what they can gain out of the case than actually helping me get out of situations. I don't give a damn how good he looks at the end of the day. I only care if my name stays out of the headlines and off the streets.

"I'll settle down when you tell me I'm not going to end up in prison."

"Trust me on this. I am an expert at negotiation. I'll make absolutely sure you won't go to prison." His voice hangs in the air, suggesting he wants to say something else, but can't find the words.

"And?"

He clears his throat.

"Larry, you aren't doing either one of us any good by keeping secrets from me. Can you keep me out of prison or not? If I end up incarcerated after you tell me I'm not, rest assured there will be hell to pay when I get out."

"Well, that's the thing. You can stay out of prison, but I need your full authorization to act as I see fit," he says.

"Meaning?"

"Since you will not show up to any of your trials, you have to trust that I can work things out on your behalf. No questions asked. Besides, you haven't even been convicted. We can hope that it will not come down to being guilty," Larry says optimistically.

"And what are my chances of that actually happening?"

There is another long pause on his end of the line, and I wonder how he reached the status of being the best lawyer in the Big Apple. He seems like one of the worst I've dealt with, and that is more than I care to admit.

"Larry, you aren't doing yourself any favors here."

"Slim to none. They have the bank records; they have the phone records. If you were going to get out of this, you should have covered your tracks better. But stranger things happen in the courtroom."

"Yeah, cover my tracks better. Some advice coming from a legal advisor."

"Hey, I'm trying to be as transparent as possible here. Let's be honest, you are the one who really can't afford to take this hit," Larry points out. Once more, my temper boils. I wish he was in the room with me so his face could meet my fist. Sure, that's not the best way to deal with your legal help, but he's pissing me off, and I'm Clay Jordan, I don't have to deal with this shit.

"Take care of this as quickly as possible." I'm straining not to display the tension in my voice. "Can you at least make sure that happens, or do you need someone to stay on your ass about that, too?"

"I'm working around your court dates. You want this over with yesterday but the system works differently. It may be months before something is worked out with them that satisfies everyone."

"Months?"

"It all depends on what the conviction is, what the judge offers, and what I'm allowed to take," Larry recounts. He pauses and I know he'll once more ask for my permission in a roundabout way.

"Do what you need to keep me out of jail. This shouldn't blow up and put me behind bars. If you can do that for me, I don't care how we get there."

There's a loud sigh of relief on the other end of the line and cheerfulness once more returns to my lawyer's voice. "That's what I like to hear. Mr. Jordan, your cooperation is appreciated. It'll be your best bet."

His flattery is unnecessary, his reassurance somewhat unreliable. There is enough doubt about him. Does he have what it takes to pull this off? But my business partners have told me he's good and I hope he's able to deliver on his promises.

"All right then, merry Christmas to you! I'll get back to you after Monday's court appearance." Larry's cheery voice comes through the phone.

"Fuck Christmas."

"Now who's the Scrooge here?" Larry asks, but I hang up on him. Holidays haven't mattered much to me for years. From Thanksgiving through New Year's Day, I stick my head in the sand and try to forget about the entire thing. The holidays were never a big deal in my family. My father was always gone, my mother always having an affair with another man and never home.

I was alone, and it's better that way now.

My fingers intertwine and my head listlessly turns to the window, watching the snowflakes fall from the sky. From thirty stories up, they have a long way before they land on the street below.

I bury my face in my hands and take a deep breath. Perhaps Larry will come through and this nightmare will all go away.

How he does it is not important—I just can't go to prison.

2

ALEXIS

"Sir, would you donate a dollar to the Alyssa's Friends Foundation? It's a nonprofit meant to—okay. Oh, miss! Excuse me, would you like to donate a dollar to the Alyssa's Friends Foundation? No? Okay, merry Christmas anyway." Walking back to my place in the corner of the mall, I hold my flyers and stand next to my empty table.

I sink into my seat, thinking of a new way to approach people. No one has donated in the past three days, and even before that, a measly fifty dollars has been raised so far. After several weeks, I'm stuck in the mud with the wheels spinning.

It's Christmas. It's supposed to be the season of giving, yet I'm watching the shoppers walk in and out of the stores, all of them loaded up with bags of junk. The true meaning of the season has been lost on the world.

Buy what you can, show off to your friends and family with your gifts to them, eat as much as you can, drink, and it's all in the spirit of the holiday. That's not what Christmas is about—it's exhausting me.

My little station was set up here in hopes to raise money and awareness for the charity I am trying to start. As a junior in college, it's not easy to find the time to work on my own charity, or to volunteer with ones I'm already passionate about, but that doesn't stop me from trying.

Now that it's Christmas break, or rather winter break, there's more than a month to throw myself into my passion and finally get this charitable trust up and running. That is, if someone walking by my table will pay attention.

Most of the time, I just get strange looks from passersby. Often, they wave their hand and shake their head, not bothering to hear me or wish me good luck. Would any other twenty-two-year-old sacrifice their entire break to singlehandedly start a charity?

So why not spare a few moments of your time?

"Hello, sir!" I start again, seeing a prospect coming out of a store. He immediately hits the Bluetooth in his ear, and I don't know if he's really talking to someone, or if he's merely avoiding me. Either way, he's unapproachable now. The mall is very strict with their policies on who you can and can't draw near with your service and people who are on the phone, conducting business, or signaling they want to be left alone are on that list.

I sit back in my chair and look at the table in front of me. There are a few little things I've got set up, detailing my idea, as well as my upbringing. My sister Allysa's smile catches my eye.

She is the reason I want to start this foundation, and she's the reason it's going to succeed. We were twins, inseparable, identical. We loved all the same things, shared all the same secrets, and vowed we'd never be torn apart.

Yet, when we were nine years old, she was diagnosed with leukemia. It was a tough battle, and she fought with all the might she had, but after three long years of torment, countless treatments, hours at her hospital bed, and enough tears to fill the ocean, she quietly passed away the night before our twelfth birthday.

It left me devastated to this day. And there is not enough research to find a cure for this terrible disease. Sure, there are foundations and hospitals dedicated to helping children with such illness, except, for me, that is not enough. It wasn't enough for Alyssa. If more treatments were available, she might still be here today.

To me, her death is not just another statistic. Alyssa's memory will not be another sad story. My charity will make a difference, and my sister's face will be headlining it. I envision the time it will be completed and become a genuine charity: everyone in the world will know who Alyssa Simone is.

"Good evening, ma'am! Do you have a moment? Could you contribute to a humanitarian charity? It's Christmas and this is for a great cause!" An elderly woman hears as she departs from one of the most expensive stores in the mall.

"What is it?"

"Thank you, the name is Alyssa's Friends Foundation. It's for children who are battling leukemia," My heart skips a beat. "The goal is to fund more research and hopefully find a cure."

"Oh, how tender. Unfortunately, I have spent all that is possible today. Have a very merry Christmas!" and she keeps on. Something tells me to pursue her, to hound her like the men who sell the manicure kits, but I can't. She has given me her answer; although she holds hundreds of dollars' worth of absolute rubbish, she will not change her mind.

"Miss Simone, how are you today?" a voice from behind gets my attention. I turn with raised eyebrows. I recognize Mr. Scott immediately; he is the general manager of the mall. He wanders around throughout the day, talks to customers, speaks with the staff; he makes sure things go smoothly. It's rare for him to give me a second glance. Perhaps he's got some good news to share?

"Mr. Scott, it's good to see you! What can I do for you?" I ask, smiling.

"How is your fundraiser going?" He asks as he critically examines the table, lingering over the empty jar next to my sister's picture.

"It's going well," I lie.

"Uh-huh. Unfortunately, the mall has a policy if you rent a space for more than a couple of days, it should be something that generates revenue for the mall. You see, the other vendors all pay a commission on what they sell. You are not."

My heart sinks. This is the last thing I need to deal with on top of everything else.

"Oh, I didn't know that. Since it's for such a good cause, and it's Christmas, perhaps you would consider making an exception?"

"I'm afraid not. Other vendors know you aren't paying for your space. We believe in equality, which, at times, means we need to impose rules on those who aren't living up to what everyone else is doing," he replies.

"I understand, but there's no other way I can get direct contact with the public." My voice quivers.

"Rules are rules, Miss Simone. I'm afraid we will impose them or they aren't worth a thing. Either you pay for your space or pack it up."

There's no way I can afford this. I can barely make ends meet as it is. It's tough enough never to touch the money raised for the foundation. Although, my morals are high and nothing will change them. No matter how inflexible things get.

A forced smile appears on my face.

"Sure, thank you for the chance." I turn to break down the table but note a surprised look on his face. Clearly, he thought it would be more difficult to get rid of me but making a scene has never been my thing. I believe in peace, not violence, to get my point across.

"Thank you," he says. He turns to go but barely takes a few

steps before he turns once more. "You know, there is a way to make an exception."

"What do you mean?" I look up with surprise and hope.

"We are about to set up the Santa Claus display and we need a lead elf. If you are willing to take the position, you'll be contributing to the business, and you can ask the parents about donations while their children are photographed," Mr. Scott said.

"I'll take it! Thank you, thank you!"

He holds his hands up to quiet me.

"This isn't exactly protocol, but I admire what you are doing and would like to help if I can. Be here early tomorrow and we'll get you fitted into a costume. Oh, and here," he looks around to make sure no one is watching, then hands me a ten-dollar bill. "For your charity."

I smile, fighting the tears welling up in my eyes. "You have no idea what this means to me."

"Merry Christmas," he replies. He clasps his hands behind his back and walks off with the same regal attitude he always has.

"Merry Christmas," I whisper, shaking my head in disbelief. Perhaps this will be a good holiday season after all.

3

CLAY

Walking back and forth in my office, my stomach is in a knot. When will the phone ring? Larry has to tell me how the trial went but those can drag on for hours. I was more than welcome to join him but wished not to be anywhere near that courtroom.

The paparazzi will not hound me as I'm led out of the courtroom in handcuffs. Too many celebrities have been in that situation for me to recognize that that will not be me. I've been in and out of scraps with the law before, but never gotten locked up for it.

"Mr. Morgan is on line one, Mr. Clay," my secretary interrupts over the intercom.

"Take a message, please."

"He says it's urgent."

"I said take a damn message!" I speak so loudly she can hear it on the other side of the glass office. She looks in my direction. I will not make eye contact. She's on my payroll, not the other way around.

I call the shots around here. If she has a problem with that, she knows where the exit is. My staff members are expected to obey me as soon as the order is given. Without question, without delay, and certainly with no argument. Great privilege comes with being the boss, and I take full advantage of it.

My thoughts wander back to the trial. Once again, the knot returns to my stomach. There is no way to eavesdrop on what is being discussed. What is Larry telling them?

Will they convict me? Is there a plea deal? He was adamant that I should trust him. What is up his sleeve? But again, all my business partners affirm he's the best of the best and say to trust him.

"Pardon me, Mr. Clay, someone is here to see you," my secretary's voice comes through the intercom again.

"Damn it, Claire! I told you to fucking leave me alone until I say otherwise! Is that difficult to understand?"

"I understand, sir. I wasn't sure if that also meant those who are here in person," she replies with uncertainty in her voice.

"Leave me alone means leave me the fuck alone!"

"What would you like me to tell them?"

"To go to hell." She's looking toward me once again but has the sense not to glare. She rises from her seat and disappears around the corner, probably to get rid of the unwelcome visitor.

I don't give a damn who has come to see me. Anything they want can wait at least until this afternoon. How can Claire can be so stupid at times? I really question whether it was a good idea to give her the position.

At the time, it was her décolletage that sold me. I never touch her, but the daily eye candy is enough to put up with her incompetence.

Shaking my head, I resume walking back and forth, my hands clasped behind my back, my head held high. Anyone looking into my office might think I'm making some great business decision, or grappling with an offer for some investment. The employees do not know what's really going on with me, or that my sweaty palms and slow breathing are indicative of my nerves.

My personal phone rings. slightly startling me. It's rare for me to be anxious but I'm so on edge, it does not take much today. My temper is flaring over every little thing, and I lack patience for any kind of stupidity. Or any interaction, for that matter.

I see it's Larry calling and quickly answer.

"Larry, how did it go?" The words fly out of my mouth before he has a chance to greet me.

"In some ways better than expected; in other ways not so great." I roll my eyes and let out a loud, exasperated sigh. He always beats around the bush, never giving a clear answer.

"What's the verdict? Am I going to prison or not?"

"That is why I'm saying things didn't quite go as well as we would have hoped." His tone is hard to read. My heart races and the knots in my stomach grow. This is the worst-case scenario and the nastiest thing about it is the fact there is no way to change it.

"What do you mean? It seems like a simple enough question to me, so please give me a simple answer. Am I going to go to prison or not?"

"In spite of a long battle, the jury returned with a guilty verdict. And we put forth enough evidence for reasonable doubt, but the case is nevertheless closed."

"Fuck!" So I'm going to prison? "Fucking great, Larry! You get one job to do and you fuck the whole thing up! How you had to do it was not important! You could not even achieve that."

He mumbles, but it's too upsetting. "How long will they lock me up for? Huh? What is the fine they imposed? Surely you need to be paid for your incompetence, regardless."

Larry at last musters up his words, cutting into my rant.

"Hold on there, Clay. I said they gave a guilty verdict, not that you were going to prison."

That sounds more hopeful than what I originally thought. "So what, then?"

"Take a deep breath and please do not interrupt me," he requests. "This will sound bad at first, but you need to trust it's all worked out."

"Give it to me, Larry; quit fucking stalling!"

"With a guilty verdict came a five-year prison sentence."

"Larry!"

"Hold on, do not interrupt me. I asked for your full permission to work out anything I could. There was a reason." My heart is racing and it's tricky to control my breathing.

"Meaning?"

"We struck a plea deal. You might not like it, but it's better than an orange jumpsuit."

"What is it? Get to the point already!"

"It turns out that the Berkshire Mall has been struggling lately. And they need a Santa Claus for the kids this month."

"What the hell?"

"You will fill the part, but you will do it out of the goodness of your heart. Any proceeds—and trust me, a Santa isn't cheap—will go back to the mall, to keep it going, you see?" Larry announces cheerfully. "You did not want a suit at all, but wouldn't you rather take Saint Nick over prison stripes?"

"I hate Christmas, and I hate children. How the hell am I going to pull this off? Is there something else I can do?" I asked with a tone of indignation.

"Go to prison," Larry replies dryly. "If you don't fulfill this—meaning you have to be there every single day, from the time it opens to the time it closes, living to the standard of the company, then you will go to prison."

"Dammit."

"It's a pretty sweet deal, actually."

"How the hell do they consider this worth five years of prison? Just out of curiosity."

"The mall is a historical landmark, Clay. No one wants to see it go under. Besides the greedy corporate businesses, no offense. You will go there first thing in the morning. A special clock in and clock out code will prove your requirements are fulfilled. Then you go home, crack open a beer, and count the days until Christmas."

"Great. That sounds so jolly."

"That's the spirit!" Larry intentionally ignores my tone. "Trust me, Clay, this is the best option. And who knows? It might do you some good."

"I highly doubt that."

"One thing's for sure," he says in his still annoyingly enthusiastic tone.

"What's that?"

"You're going to look forward to Christmas!"

4

ALEXIS

"How do I look?" I ask with a wide smile. My elf outfit is adorable, and I'm even more thrilled to get the chance to promote my charity while guiding the children and their parents to Santa.

"You look great! Let's just hope our Santa actually shows up," Mr. Scott comments. As usual, he's standing with his arms clasped behind his back and surveying the busy room. The mall isn't doing as well as it could be financially, but there are still many people milling about.

Some stop to look at the sign we've set up next to Santa's chair. The children are all very excited to see him, though there are still some parents who don't look entirely thrilled. This might be hectic. There will be a lot of parents eager to get it over with, and they will push and pull, getting their kids to the front of the line.

I've never helped with anything like this before. Hopefully I can manage it without much trouble.

"I hope he does, too," I reply. "Although it didn't sound like he had much of a choice from what you mentioned."

"He'll be here if he wants to stay out of jail," Mr. Scott replies.

That makes me chuckle and he gives me a confused look. "What's so funny?"

"It's rather strange we're using someone who broke the law as our Santa Claus. It just seems a little ironic."

He smirks and nods. "I agree with you on that one."

"Tell me again who he is. His name sounds familiar."

"Clay Jordan," Mr. Scott says with a shrug. "He did something with his finances and the IRS found out. It's redundant. Let's just hope enough parents bring their kids to see him so we can make some money."

"Plenty of people will be here. After all, who wouldn't want to bring their kid to see one of the richest people in New York?"

"You have to keep that in check," Mr. Scott reminds me. "This is Santa Claus we're talking about, and the kids will have to be sold on that."

"Once he puts on the suit, he'll be the jolly old Saint Nick we need him to be," I say optimistically. "After all, he's trying to stay out of jail, right?"

"That's something else you need to keep to yourself!" Mr. Scott calls out over his shoulder as he walks away. "This is meant to be professional!"

I roll my eyes. Being professional is not a problem and it happens when I feel like it. Except, I will not pretend this guy impresses me. He's not doing this because he wants to. He is being forced into it. He's just a spoiled rich brat and someone I prefer not to be involved with more than what is necessary.

I might be the head elf, but my focus will be on spreading the word about my foundation and promoting my sister's memory. Who cares if some rich guy is here while I do it?

Maybe he'll actually draw a crowd big enough that the donations are bigger.

"And this is Alexis. She'll be working with you and keeping the kids in check," Mr. Scott announces as he returns.

"You must be Clay." I hold my hand out to the stranger next to him.

"I am," he says shortly.

"Alexis will show you the dressing room where you'll find the suit. It's hanging up inside. I hope it fits," Mr. Scott cuts in again. I smirk, not at all hiding the fact that I'm staring at this guy's body. He is a lot more attractive than I imagined and I like what I'm looking at.

He's a typical tall, dark, and handsome guy and something about the look on his face screams that he is wealthy. He's clearly not hurting for confidence, either, and he openly looks me over as well.

"Shall we?" I motion for him to follow me. He walks with the same confidence and I square my shoulders, taking the lead. I feel Mr. Scott staring at us but I don't turn around. He's clearly impressed with this man. There are plenty of people out there who need money, and this greedy man committed some tax fraud to keep more than he should.

At least, that's my judgment.

"The suit is hanging up inside. Just put it on and come back out to find me. We still have a few things to do before we can lower the ropes for the kids," I say with a toss of my hair.

"Are we doing that today?" he asks with annoyance in his voice.

"Today we need to set everything up. You will help, of course, but you're also going to smile and wave at the kids. We are not officially opening the lines until tomorrow, but that doesn't mean we can't drum up some excitement," I say with a sly grin.

Looks like he doesn't want to be here, and I'm going to eat up every moment of it. This will not only do him good, but it will be nice to watch someone who is so full of themselves be open and welcome to people he would not give a second glance on the street.

"Great," he replies.

"Just get into the suit and find me. If it doesn't fit, we'll be able to work around it. But it looks like it'll be fine. Here you go!" I hand him the fat suit with another grin and Clay snatches it out of my hand.

"I'm looking forward to it," I say, walking out of the room.

I'm going to enjoy this way more than I should.

5

CLAY

I don't have high expectations for how this will turn out. I don't want to be here and I have made that utterly clear to everyone involved. Scott is someone I've crossed paths with before and he's all right. I'm not sure about this sassy brunette he's got working with me, nonetheless.

She hasn't spoken about her past or the reason for being here, though I get the feeling she's one of those women who gets involved with charities and the spirit of the season. Not that I disagree that the world should be nicer, but I'll never like this time of year and I'm not afraid to point that out to anyone who listens.

"How's it going?" Mr. Scott asks as he walks up. "Are you all ready to have those kids telling you what they want from Santa this year?"

"As ready as I'll ever be," I reply, shaking my head. "This is the weirdest sentence I've ever had."

"I don't know much about your situation, obviously, but this will be a lot better than jail. You don't want to spend Christmas behind bars, do you?"

"I can't say it would bother me much." Scott gives me a sidelong glance. He's trying to figure out if I'm serious or not. Oh well, I'll let him wonder. It's true, it's better to avoid having another scandal on my record or having a ton of fines.

If this is the way to stay out, then I'll put up with it. I Not necessarily happily, but I'll put up with it.

"I hear some reporters will be here today," Scott continues.

"Reporters?" The displeasure shows in my tone.

"Do you think we won't be hit with those who try to capture the warm fuzzy feeling for the rest of the city? Come on, you know how they are." Scott gives me another strange look.

"Again, I can't say it's thrilling."

"Oh, come on, it's not so bad. Why don't you embrace this? Be the guy who loves giving back to his community! People go crazy for things like that," Scott reminds me.

"Whatever for?"

"Because you know how gossip works. If any of the parents recognize you, they will talk. Give them something good to talk about!" he suggests.

I roll my eyes. "Let's hope no one recognizes me. How about that?"

"Sure, you can hope for that, but if you're working with Alexis I wouldn't plan on remaining completely anonymous," he teases. "It might take some convincing on her end."

"She seems far more worried about convincing the kids. What is her deal anyway? Is she one of those super charities?"

"Sort of. She's trying to get her own organization off the ground. Not many people are willing to give her donations and she's having a tough time. I let her work here and promote her charity as long as she draws people in," Scott explained. "Although, in reality, a lot of the work is going to fall on you."

"What sort of charity is that?" My tone is mocking. "Is she saving puppies from a shelter? To make sure they all have a home by Christmas?"

"That wouldn't be too far off the mark, but no. It's something in memory of her sister. Leukemia, I believe it was," Scott says as he looks down at his phone. "Excuse me, I really need to take this."

He walks away, putting the phone up to his ear. A part of me feels like an ass for making fun of Alexis' charity. She strikes me as someone more worried about the puppies and kittens than anything that is truly an issue in the world.

"Will you stand there all day, or are you coming up to see the kids?" Alexis' voice fills the air behind me and I turn. She looks me over from head to toe. "I guess you'll have to do."

I slip the beard over my face, adjusting it in the mirror before turning back to her. "Aren't you supposed to be getting the crows psyched or something? You are the preppy one in this operation."

"I don't care to be referred to as preppy, and they are pretty excited as it is. My job is to make sure you hold up your end of the bargain," she says, putting her hand on her hips. "It might surprise you how much your performance report depends on my findings."

She gets me chuckling. "Mr. Scott asked you to motivate me? Because I know Larry wouldn't have come to you in a million years, especially not for something like this."

"What you think of me is irrelevant, but please treat me with more respect than that. I'm capable of supervising you and a lot of other things," she retorts.

"So I hear." She looks at my smirk questioningly but I ignore her. The last thing I want is for her to try to hit me up as a sponsor. My company does not do that shit, and she won't go crying to Mr. Scott about something petty on my account.

Of course, he can't force me to hand her my money, but he might make this go as roughly for me as possible.

"Okay, Santa Claus. When we get out there, you are the

chubby guy in the red suit. A lot of little kids want to see you, tell you what they want for Christmas, and renew their faith that you exist," Alexis says as we walk through the hall.

"As if they need that sort of reassurance."

"How old were you when you quit believing in Santa?" she shoots back.

"Oh, I never did. My parents were always upfront and practical with me and didn't lie to me about the presents under the tree" I reply with a nonchalant shrug. She laughs, and it seems she's laughing at me more than anything.

"That's one of the most pathetic things I've ever heard. It's not lying to your kids; it's believing in a greater good. By the looks of it, you could definitely use some of that." She shakes her head with a bemused look on her face. I suddenly want to shove her against the wall.

It's difficult enough! She's so good looking, but all that sass makes it difficult to stay focused around her. There are many women in my life, and I can take any one of them to bed.

Nevertheless, something about Alexis makes me think she wouldn't be so effortless. In fact, I get the impression she'd like the thrill of the chase but she'd complicate things to make any real advances on her.

And that only makes me want her more. This woman will be in my bed—that will happen. She'll play hard to get, but the way she looks at me gives me a sense of what's going on in her head. She doesn't want to admit it, but she likes me.

She desires me.

"Try to make this believable," she says as I hold out my arms to the cheering children. I turn so my back is to the crowd as I start up the stairs.

"Just try to keep up," I smirk.

6
ALEXIS

By the end of the week, everything has gone better than I thought it would. Clay seems to make the effort, at least to the kids' faces. At times he has a look on his face that proves how little he wants to be there, but he doesn't want more trouble with the law, so he endures it.

"Thank God it's just an hour until closing," I say, looking at the clock. It takes effort to be a little easier to get along with, though it's far from easy being around him. He's an arrogant asshole and does not hold back from that fact when we're alone.

Sometimes it seems like he's flirting with me, then other times it's obvious he just wants to get in my pants. And neither is going to happen.

He can flirt all he likes, but I don't respond and will not. He's much older than me— some fifteen years. He comes from a world of selfishness and greed, while my life has been dedicated to helping people.

He borderline mocks me when we're unaccompanied— acting like my work is a lost cause. People like him are part of what is wrong with this world. He needs to pull his head out of his ass and realize there are more people on the planet than him.

"Glad to hear that," he replies without looking up.

"Are you going to the party tomorrow?" I ask, trying to sound uncaring.

"Party?" he replies.

He is fully aware of the party. Mr. Scott has invited the entire staff in the mall. It sounds like it'll be a lot of fun. I like the kinds of parties that aren't upper class. The ones where people can cut loose and have some fun without having to stand on ceremony to impress anyone.

"I take it you're going?" Clay reverses the subject.

"Of course. These people are my friends," I reply tartly. "But if you're too good to be around us, it's probably best you stay home."

"I didn't say a thing about staying home. What makes you think this is a party I want to attend when there are countless other events I've been invited to? Don't get me wrong, I'm sure it's going to be cute, but it's not my scene." Clay's tone is insulting.

"Cute is not how one would describe it. Mr. Scott does a great job planning these things every year. This is the first time I can be present at it, and I look forward to it." I stamp my foot on the ground after saying it.

Clay looks at me, amused. He's clearly hitting my buttons and enjoying doing it. I have to be careful not to give him details or show weakness. This guy will use it to his advantage.

The rest of the evening passes quickly. We finish with the set and Clay gets ready to go to the dressing room but I push my way past him.

"Whoa, someone is in a hurry," he says with another grin. "It might appear you don't want to talk to me."

"I don't. People who are too good to hang out with others aren't worth my time. My life's work is to make sure everyone is treated fairly in this world. It's people like you who make that difficult."

My hands are on my hips as I'm speaking. He laughs and, immediately, my cheeks flush crimson. Why is this man getting under my skin so much?

"What's so funny?"

"You," he replies with a shake of his head. I open my mouth to get more details, but Mr. Scott interrupts us.

"The two of you should know that we've been doing better this year than we have in ages," he says with a grin.

"That's great!" I say enthusiastically, turning to face him. Clay will get the cold shoulder, and he'll see I can be warm and welcoming. If he's going to be difficult, then he'll wind up alone.

"Did you hear about the party we're having tomorrow night?" Mr. Scott turns his attention to Clay. "You should come; you are part of the reason we're doing so well. Actually, you are most of the reason."

"Clay isn't sure he can spare the time with the likes of us," I answer. "We were talking about that very issue."

"Oh really? That is a shame. If you change your mind, we're going to have a lot of food, a lot of booze, and a lot of conversation," Mr. Scott says, smiling. Can he tell how much I dislike Clay? Or rather, how much I try to dislike him?

"I'll think about it," he replies, and the two shake hands.

"I'll be there," I volunteer with a grin. "We know how to have a good time."

"I look forward to it," Mr. Scott says with a smile. I give Clay another look before heading back to get my things. I just wear the elf dress to work. I don't mind looking like an elf when my shift is over. The people seem to like it.

Walking to my locker to get my purse, I feel Clay's eyes glued on me. What is going on in his mind? His gaze is so penetrating, it seems he can look into my very soul. I fight to keep from blushing every time he does so, and it seems he knows he's doing it.

He's not the type of guy who is intimidated by women. Let alone a woman like me. But he doesn't need to know that. I ignore him on my way back out the door, eager to make it to my car before he comes out to the parking lot.

There are times he's not hitting on me openly, more than likely because we are on the clock, and I have no clue what I'd do if he did. It would be tough not to be receptive to it, although I still am determined just to ignore him.

I start my car with a sigh and let it warm up in the bitter cold. Clay comes out but he doesn't wait for his car to warm before he pulls out and drives away. Sitting in my parked car, I stare after him as he drives up the street and vanishes out of sight.

I admit, I really hope he comes to the party. I don't want to even act like I care, and I'm not going to. Clay might be able to seduce the world, but if there's one thing he won't do is read me. Even with a stone-cold poker face, when it comes to him and his interest in me, it will not be reciprocated.

He might have glanced in his rearview mirror as he drove away. My heart races and a wave of excitement washes over me. I've had suitors in the past, but no one with the same kind of attitude Clay Jordan has.

He looks at me so intently. It is so primal, it sends waves of anticipation through my entire body.

I put my car into drive, shaking my head and slowly make my own way out of the icy parking lot. What has come over me? What have I been thinking?

That man is here temporarily. More than likely, we'll never see each other again at the end of the month. We are nothing more than two volunteers. Well, one of us is voluntary, anyway. The looks and the flirting might add to the excitement but will not go further than that.

As he commented—we come from two different worlds.

7
CLAY

I finish adjusting my tie, looking in the mirror, but cannot decide where to go. There are plenty of holiday parties, many of them laden with champagne, beautiful women, and business connections. I planned on going to Harley Mann's party down at the bank. He is one of the wealthiest men and he can be helpful in getting me out of this scrape.

For some odd reason, the party at the mall keeps returning to my mind. What would be appealing about it? On paper, absolutely nothing.

In reality, a young woman is possessing me.

How she treated me the day before about the event was incredibly erotic. She does not seem the kind of a woman to back down and apparently she doesn't care who I am. By the looks she gives me throughout the day, or when she turns her face away every time I give her a compliment, she wants me.

I know she does.

I can go to any party and the odds are in my favor I'll be going home with a woman. However, I don't want to go home with any woman—I want to take Alexis home with me. I want to lay her on the bed and show her how skilled my mouth is and what it means to be fucked properly.

She's young. noticeably inexperienced, and I want to be the first to really blow her mind.

What is her experience, anyhow?

My phone chimes. My driver has arrived. Whoever I end up seeing, I plan on getting merry and won't deal with driving back on the icy roads. Walking down the stairs, my mind is still spinning with indecisiveness and it's not until the cab driver asks for the destination that I can give an answer.

"What the hell? Take me down to the Berkshire Mal."

He gives me a look. He's driven for me before, and he's aware of the parties I like to attend. The Berkshire is definitely out of character but he knows better than to comment.

We ride along in silence and I stare out the window at the swirling snow. It's already dark, but the lights capture the tiny flakes and glint with sparkles. It's peaceful, but I can't shake my disdain for this time of year. New York gets cold, and I'm beyond ready for the holidays to be over and summer to return.

"There you go, mate," my driver says, bringing me back to the moment.

"Thank you." I pay him and slip out of the vehicle. Why am I feeling nervous? I never feel nervous but right now there are butterflies in my stomach and my palms are getting damp. These are folks I would never associate with but there is a particular woman I really want to see.

"Clay! You made it!" Mr. Scott walks over with rosy cheeks and a glass of champagne in his hand. "I didn't think you were coming, but you son of a gun, you made it!"

"I might not stay long. Several other venues may require my attention," I say quickly. "But it won't hurt me to stop by for a few minutes."

"Excellent. Help yourself to the champagne and food. Of

course, mingle your little heart out as well; you don't have to sit on that throne tonight!" he points to the seat behind him. I smile silently. I want to ask him if he knows where Alexis is, but that's not really my style. If she's around, she'll notice me at some point.

And I'm right.

"Well, look who graced us meek mortals with his presence," she says coolly as she walks over, a glass of champagne in her hand as well. She's in her twenties but still looks out of place with alcohol in her hand. As though she's too young, or perhaps, too innocent?

"I thought I'd see how things were getting on here. Care to walk me to the champagne table?"

She looks surprised and distrustful. Looking at the glass in her hand, she swirls the liquid and shrugs. "It's not like you can't find it yourself."

"No, but if I came to socialize, it won't do me much good to lean back in a corner, will it?" She gives me another look. Distrust is still on her face. She's probably worried I'll ask her out. And perhaps not because of the question itself but due to what her response will be.

"Come on, then." She doesn't bother to hide her annoyance. Something about it makes it feigned. She's not attempting to annoy me; she's not bothered. In fact, she's putting up a wall to defend against her own feelings.

We walk over to the table and I grab one of the glasses, turning to her and swirling it in my hand like a gentleman. She's checking out my suit, and I take the moment to openly compliment her gown.

"It's tough to recognize you when you're not dressed like an elf." She blushes but tries to look exasperated.

"I don't always wear that outfit."

"Good. Because you look much better in this."

"And you look a lot better in a Santa suit, if you ask me," she says with a mischievous grin. My heart skips a beat. I knew she'd flirt if we were alone.

"Why do you say that? Not a fan of nice abs?" I ask, patting my stomach. She visibly blushes and looks away. She's probably wondered what was hidden under my shirt all this time.

"Not exactly what I was getting at." She's not hiding the sheepish grin on her face.

I'm about to ask her what she meant, when we are interrupted by Mr. Scott.

"Oh dear! Everyone! What did I tell you?" he calls out. We look at him in surprise. He points above our heads. "I knew this was the best place to catch a duo eventually!"

We look up and Alexis gasps. We are directly below a mistletoe, something I didn't even think to check when we walked over to the table. By Alexis' reaction, she also had no idea that it was there.

"You know what that means!" Scott presses. "Both of you owe us a kiss!"

"Oh, I don't know about that," Alexis argues, "Won't it be weird if we have to work together again?"

"Kiss! Kiss! Kiss! Kiss!" Scott starts chanting, and it's not long before the rest of the room joins in. Alexis looks undecided. This is my chance. I put the champagne on the table and turn to take her in my arms. She doesn't fight me. In fact, she is trembling beneath my touch, her body full of anticipation.

My own arousal is tough to subdue in my own pants. There is no doubt what her desires are. If there was a way to rip her clothes off and take her on the table right now ... That is a fantasy for sure.

I press my lips to hers and she lets out a slight moan. It's soft enough no one else hears it, but her flushing cheeks tell me she didn't mean to let it out. She looks embarrassed as she pulls away from me. They are all cheering.

It's so effortless to entertain people with champagne in them.

"I have to go," Alexis says softly. She grabs her glass of champagne and disappears into the crowd. I don't follow her. The way she reacted to my kiss, it's just a matter of time before we catch up again. It's better not to bring it up. It's the first step to what I want to do with her.

Perhaps my wish of taking her home with me tonight will come true after all.

It will be a Christmas miracle.

8

ALEXIS

Rushing to the back room, praying Clay doesn't follow me, I am angry with myself for not noticing the mistletoe hanging above the table. Mr. Scott told me earlier he would hide it in the room and we agreed we'd abide by the rules if we were caught beneath it.

To be fair, standing under there with Clay never crossed my mind. It was a surprise he showed up. I certainly didn't think we would be together when the plant was revealed.

I drain the rest of my champagne and throw away the glass, pushing my way through the door and into the dressing room. I hold my breath for a moment to hear if anyone else is there. My heart races and with shaky hands, I pull out my phone.

"Hello?" the voice on the other end of the line sounds sleepy.

"Sarah? Do you have a minute?"

"For what?"

She's groggy. Has she had a few too many herself?

"Where are you?" I ask, not answering her question.

"I just got home. That party was wild!" she says, sounding a little more awake now. "Where are you? What's going on?"

"I'm at the party at work. Well, I'm in the dressing room. I just got caught under the mistletoe." I hold my breath once more, still listening to see if I'm alone.

"Oh? Hopefully with some hottie," she teases. "Oh fuck! You didn't get stuck under there with Mr. Scott, did you? He'd love that."

I chuckle. "Of course not! But I almost would have preferred to get stuck with him."

"Who? The janitor?"

"You aren't being helpful."

"All right, all right, no more teasing. Seriously though, who was it?"

"Mr. Jordan."

"What the fuck? You got to make out with one of the richest men in the city?! How was it?"

"You don't get it! The guy is here on criminal charges. He's here because he didn't want to go to jail! I can't get involved with him! Not to mention he's like fifteen years older!"

"What is the big deal? He's gorgeous, and if you got to make out with him, take it as an accomplishment. I'd love to be caught in that situation."

I roll my eyes. Sarah has always been more open with her sex life. Even when we were in high school, she did what she could to get with the teachers. Apparently she did it on more than one occasion, though it is hard for me to know if she is lying.

"I don't want to get involved with him."

"All right, then don't." The sleepy sound returns to her voice.

"It's not that simple!"

"Why not? Oh," she says. "You like him, don't you?"

"Not like that!" I protest a little too quickly.

She chuckles once more. "You always do this. Why not cut loose and have some fun? Who knows, you might end up with a nice paycheck after this."

"You are of no help," I sigh.

"Well, I have had a lot of fun tonight. You should get back out there and see if you can lure him under the mistletoe again. Have some excitement for once in your life," Sarah says yawningly. I will not get much else out of her, so I hang up with another sigh.

Sarah has been one of my closest friends since grade school but she's also trouble and not the best person to get wholesome advice from. That doesn't stop me from going to her whenever I am in some trouble, but she always tells me the same thing.

Cut loose and have some fun.

But then, she doesn't live the same way I do. She'd be thrilled to find some sugar daddy to care of her. She has little ambition to pursue a career or make a name for herself. She wants to be taken care of, and she doesn't understand why I don't feel the same.

"Alexis?" Mr. Scott's voice fills the dressing room. "Are you in here?"

"Yeah, I had to make a quick phone call," I say hurriedly, stepping out of my stall.

"Is everything okay?" There is concern on his face but it's tainted with alcohol. I can probably tell him just about anything right now and he likely won't remember it in the morning.

"Of course, I just get overwhelmed with all the people out there, that's all," I say with a grin. "Now let's go party!"

He relaxes and puts his arm around me as we head back. "I can't believe the turnout! Can you believe Clay came?"

"It is a surprise," I say, blushing. "I hope he's having a good time."

"He had to leave. Said there was some other business to attend to," Mr. Scott sighed. "I wish he could be convinced to get more invested in this place."

"He said there isn't much to offer him here," I say without

thinking. There's a look of disappointment on Mr. Scott's face. "Of course, he's not the sort of man to look at what really matters."

"Perhaps he'll come around before the season is over," Mr. Scott replies hopefully I have my own doubts about Clay, so do not say a word. I wish he hadn't left. Or that I hadn't run following the kiss. It'll be awkward the next time we meet. He'll probably make some comment that'll make me uncomfortable and I'll have to pretend like it's nothing.

It was nothing, wasn't it?

Was he able to feel my body shiver at his touch, or were my lips trembling when they met with his? The entire situation was so erotic. It'll replay over and over throughout the night—dreams of him and how he tasted.

"Oh good, you didn't leave!" Buddy, the janitor, says as he walks over. He has champagne in his hand but nods toward the table, seeing I do not. "Do you want to get some more champagne?"

I laugh, shaking my head. "That's subtle, Buddy. I've been caught under the mistletoe enough for one night."

"Dammit. I hoped you wouldn't see through that trick." He shakes his head. "I can't get anyone to go over there with me now."

"I'd be surprised if anyone else gets caught under there again," I say with a chuckle. "That was a little surprise for all of us."

"It was nice to watch." His eyes linger and I excuse myself. It's been no secret over the past couple weeks what he wants to do with me. He's much older and very not my type. I flirt with him because it's safe and fun but have no intentions of taking it further. I won't get caught under a stupid mistletoe again.

I mingle, keeping the conversation going while avoiding talking about the kiss with Clay, but it's difficult at times. Several staff members tell me it's clear there's chemistry between us, and I can't help but wonder how obvious it is.

Who is the bigger offender? Clay has an open, intimidating attitude. I, on the other hand, prefer the softer approach, and try to treat everyone equally.

There are still plenty of giggles and glances cast my way. It has everything to do with what occurred next to the champagne table.

And no one seems surprised.

9
CLAY

"I honestly don't give a fuck what you have to say. It was agreed I was going to be there for a month doing this fucking volunteering and that's the end!" I want to hang up the phone, but have to listen to the rest of what Larry has to say.

"That's what we agreed upon, but please understand when more things come to light, we have to readdress the issue." He's speaking calmly, but the usual cheerfulness is not there.

"You said you'd take care of that!"

"I thought so too. That was before another one of your partners stepped forward with information about some foreign trades."

"What the fuck are you talking about?" For the first time in a long time, I really have no idea. I did some things, but those were all taken care of. At least, they should have been.

"Look, this is something I'm currently looking into. Keep doing what you do and if there is more, we'll get it handled then." Larry's voice has returned to being optimistic but I still want to reach through the phone and punch him.

"You can't call me up with this information and assume I'm

able to get back to work. Do you have any idea how hard it is to sit here dealing with these little brats, knowing I'm stuck here for another few weeks?"

"Oh, it can't be that bad. I love kids," he replies.

I roll my eyes. "Then why aren't you the one down here in a fucking suit?"

"Because I'm not the one with the plea deal. That's all on you." Larry laughs again. "You are doing great, I can say that much. My money was on the fact you would bail out after a day."

"Thanks for the vote of confidence."

"Anyway, you'll be in the loop on what's going on. We'll get this sorted out in no time! I'm sure we'll get it figured out in the next couple weeks."

"You better. I'm getting dreadfully tired of this entire fiasco."

"Then make sure there is nothing else that will come to light. In fact, why don't you give up on foreign trading and focus on what's right here? That mall is going under and unfortunately, the numbers still do not add up. You could buy them out and set up something new."

"That is not a bad idea, but what will that do to Mr. Scott?"

"Don't get all soft on me now, Clay. The end game is money, just like it's always been. If we can sweep this under the rug and get everyone to focus on the next great thing you could do with that space, we'll be in a good spot."

He's right. I don't want to deal with foreign trading anymore. It's too much of a headache with so many key players and I wish not to get involved in more scandals. My company is known for that, so those are the people I tend to attract.

If I were to buy out the land for this mall, I could tear it down and put up something new. Perhaps a car dealership or something to attract more investors.

"You should think about it. There's a mountain of paperwork

to get through, not to mention some people, thanks to you." Larry's voice brings me back to the present and I sigh.

"Don't go too crazy buying. This can't turn into something else," I warn.

"You know I wouldn't do that. Now get out there and enjoy the holiday spirit!" Larry laughs. "Ho ho ho!"

I hang up without responding. He's exasperating, to say the least, but he still might be helpful. I dismiss what he said about the mall. Admittedly, I've grown to care about some of the folks and don't want to upset them.

It won't be easy, however, to get out of the legal trouble I'm in. It was too good to be true to get charity duty for a month. Of course, the entire plan was to save the mall. Now I'm thinking of being the person to step in and tear it down.

"There you are! Come on, break time is over," Alexis says, poking her head into the break room. "The kids out there want to see you."

"I'm coming," I say a little too harshly. She looks at me with wide eyes then turns and walks away. She's been rather odd since the party. It probably has something to do with our kiss. But she doesn't want to talk about it. When Scott brings it up, she merely ignores it.

There's no time to deal with that right now, anyhow. Far bigger things need to be taken care of, starting with what to do with the mall. I have a few weeks to think about it, and with Larry working out the details, there's time to sit and reflect. How to approach Scott with the offer?

Unless Larry plays the bad guy.

I pull on the beard and adjust it over my face with a sigh. It's strange seeing myself in the mirror dressed up like Santa. The suit makes me look the part, but I'm not in the mood. I'm never in the mood. This isn't the kind of life cut out for me, so why the fuck am I so torn about my next business endeavor?

In all honesty, I don't really have to give Scott an offer. When it comes down to it, if he's losing the mall to a bank, all I have to do is step in and give them a bid they can't refuse. Sure, it's not the best way to handle this shit, but it's the way I know, and it's relatively painless for me.

"They'll be fine," I mutter, adjusting the suit under the beard. "It's about time the old man moves on with his life anyway."

I don't look at myself as I turn to leave. It's appalling that I'm torn about this. I should forget about personal feelings and do what is best for my company. People like Alexis and Scott are good at bouncing back after they deal with hardship. They'll be fine.

Don't get caught up with feelings for anyone.

I have to take care of myself.

10

ALEXIS

"What does that mean for us?" The worry shows in my voice. I had my hopes up so high for the charity and working with the mall that I planned on asking Mr. Scott if I can continue after the holidays with a booth of my own. Then, out of the blue, he called a business meeting and announced the mall was going under.

"Nothing yet. The plan is to make sure we work as hard as we can and bring in as much revenue as possible," he sighs. "We are doing a great job getting the people here with Santa Claus but that is not enough. The first week was great. Since then it's just gone back to the way it was."

"You've been the owner of this place for years. How can you just let it go like this?" I ask.

"It's not that simple," he replies.

I open my mouth to respond, but Buddy interrupts. "This happened to me and my family's mechanical business years ago. My father, his father, all the way up the line. But when times got tough, there wasn't much we could do about it."

"What do you mean?" I ask. The sting of tears forms in my eyes, and there's a lump in my throat.

"I mean, when you get the big corporations sweeping down out of the sky like vultures, there's not a lot you can do," Buddy attests with a bit of frustration. He's still hurt about losing his business. It's something he's brought up more than once, though no one feels comfortable inquiring about the details.

"Can't you say no?" I ask, turning my attention back to Mr. Scott.

"That's just it. When you don't have money to pay the bank and someone else does, you don't have many options," he sadly declares.

"That's bullshit!" I spit. "What do you have to say about this? You're one of those big corporations, so isn't there something we can do?"

I turn my attention to Clay, who's been sitting quietly during the whole meeting. He looks pained at my question, but recovers quickly and merely shrugs it off. "I don't deal with this sort of issue. My lawyers and a legal team work out the details so I can focus on the growth within the company."

I give him a doubtful look as if he's lying. He is the one with money and the big business, after all. It would only make sense for him to have the answer.

"Lawyers, the bane of my existence," Mr. Scott sighed. "I can't tell you how many times I've wanted to throw them out of the mall just knowing who they are."

"I can't say they're my favorite people on the planet either," Clay chimes in. He gives me a look as he speaks and I drop his gaze. I don't believe him, and unlike Mr. Scott, I won't get caught up in his lies. I'll call him out on them anytime.

"But what does that mean for all the stores here? I had plans to move forward with my work as soon as the holidays were over," I say with the lump returning to my throat.

Mr. Scott clears his throat. "If we go under, then we all have to figure out what is next on the agenda. I'm sorry, Alexis, I really am. I thought this would work out."

"This is bullshit," I say again. I turn and walk out the door, not bothering to look at Clay. He could step in and do something, if only to give us some advice on how to fight this. I'm reeling with disappointment and worry, and don't know where to turn.

The news is a bombshell to all of us. It seemed like things were doing better. Mr. Scott appeared to be most convinced that we were going to make it. The more time I've spent around him and the mall, the more attached I've grown and the less I want to ever leave.

It's a beautiful building, and there is so much potential for growth if we could give it the facelift it needs. But now, it is too late. I barely get by on the wages he pays me, and my sister's charity is doing even worse.

But I've decided this is my second home and I have been doing everything in my power to keep it going. Now it looks like all my hard work will crumble. Mr. Scott will sell out, all my friends and colleagues will move on with their lives, and Clay Jordan will be the millionaire he's used to being.

I, on the other hand, will be back to square one. There is no future for me after this. I'll have to give up on the charity, find a new job, and once again face the reality of whether or not I can finish school.

It isn't fair.

"There you are. In your own famous words, isn't it time you get back to work?" Clay asks as he poked his head into the dressing room. "The kids out there are waiting to see me."

I give him a look. "Don't act like you give a damn about this place or anyone in it!"

"How is this my fault?" he asks coolly. "This isn't my business, and I'm only here because the judge ordered me."

"That's a large part of the problem!" I snap. "You don't care about this place anymore than you care about anything else. You live for you, and that's it!"

"Is there anyone else to live for?" I sense a nerve was hit, but it won't stop me from continuing.

"There are a lot of other people you could live for. Instead, you spend all your time going from one meaningless party to the next, never making a real connection, except for the fraud charges, maybe," I smirked.

He spins around to face me and for the first time, he's genuinely angry. "How dare you bring that up? You don't know a damn thing about that or anything else in the business world!"

"How else do you suppose I'm able to manage starting charities and work my way up the ladder any place I've ever worked?" My arms cross over my chest.

"For one, your charities are never successful, and working at a shopping mall for Christmas is no real achievement," Clay coldly replies. My jaw drops, and a sob dews in the back of my throat. But I'm not going to cry in front of him.

There is no way I'll ever give him that satisfaction.

"We'll be late." I push past him. I'm not the kind of woman to ever follow a man, let alone one who just treated me with such little respect. He's walking behind me and I toss my hair, causing the little bells in my ponytail to jingle happily.

I'm not sure what to do next. But, through it all, I blame Clay for some of it. He knows how to handle business, but he's throwing in the towel because he doesn't have to see the consequences.

He's right. He'll be here through the end of his sentence, then go back to the life he's used to. None of this affects him in the slightest.

I'll prove him wrong. I don't care what he has to say about

my charities, or what I'll do next. I'll prove to the entire world that I don't need anyone else to help me.

If Mr. Scott wants to let his business burn to the ground, that's up to him. I'm sick of these men who don't know how to chase what they want.

I'll show them all.

11

CLAY

It's a long afternoon. There's silence in the dressing room as I take off the suit and Alexis gathers her things. She's still pissed but for some reason, I can't find the words to apologize. She's turned this back on me when I have nothing to do with it.

But she's young and doesn't know the way of the world yet. Her ambition amazes me but she doesn't have the experience to match.

There's no denying the fact I'll be here for another couple of weeks; however, I prefer not to spend time with her being so angry. It makes it incredibly difficult to work with the kids when she has a mindset, but with her ties to Mr. Scott, there's nothing to say about it.

She gathers up her things and heads for the door.

"Look, Alexis ... What I said earlier ..." I'm terrible at apologies!

She whirls around with fire in her eyes. "I don't give a damn if you're sorry or not! Let's not talk about it! Leave me the hell alone!"

"That was a shitty thing for me to say. Let's not end our partnership ..."

She laughs. "Partnership? You are here for one reason and one reason only. Mine is completely different than yours. We might work in the same place, but we are not partners."

"Whatever you want to call it. Let's not be so tense for the next two weeks. You didn't have fun this afternoon either."

"Don't flatter yourself. You need not pay attention to me for me to have fun." Her eyebrows rise. "I'm not like the women you tend to spend time with."

"That's one of the things I admire about you. You are not like them at all." She wasn't expecting that kind of answer. "You are far more determined, and you have vision for your life. You are not the kind of woman to be flaunted."

"Hell no. I would kill a man if he ever tried to flaunt me." The fire is still blazing in her eyes.

"Which is why I want to ask if you will join me for dinner. As two respectable adults. And one being very sorry for what he said."

Her hands drop to her sides and she looks at me with shock. "Why would you think I'd want to have dinner with you?"

"Because you like to go out for dinner, and you know me."

"I know you're an asshole."

"Most people in my life are. It goes with the job description." I grin at her teasingly. She softens a bit.

"Santa Claus is not supposed to be an asshole." She's fighting a smile.

"You'd be surprised what you learn about good old Saint Nick. Many of the heroes we celebrate were kind of dicks in real life. Have you ever read up on the real one?"

"Never cared to. I like thinking of him as magical and kind to everyone," she sighs. "Realizing the real one was just a man sort of makes me sad."

"Well, he wouldn't be too happy if he knew you were sad this time of year."

She gives me another look. "Are you talking about the real one or the fake one?"

"Either one wants you to be happy," I shrug. "And why wouldn't they?"

"It's probably not a good idea." She's trying to change the subject but her expression looks agreeable.

"Come on, it's just a couple of friends having dinner. When's the last time you went anywhere you fancied?"

"Anywhere I want?" She looks at me with expectation in her eyes. "I suppose that means we'll go to a burger joint and not a five-star restaurant?"

"I love burgers. We can go anywhere you please. What I said this afternoon made me feel bad and I wish to make it up to you. You name the place and a cab will pick you up in an hour."

"I'll let you know," She gives me another strange look. I smile back.

"I'll see you in an hour."

ALEXIS THREAT for hamburgers is just that—in fact, she selects a more expensive venue. She's never gotten this before and it's delightful to show her my world.

"This is so gorgeous!" She looks around the room. "I had no idea!"

"You gave me the impression you might like it. As you mentioned you hadn't been to this particular venue, you should have a chance to try it."

"You come here often? Am I the date of the night?"

"You sound jealous," I tease. "Are you thinking about the mistletoe incident?"

"No, never," she says a little too hastily. "That was one of the most embarrassing moments I've ever had to go through."

"I thought it was nice." She gives me a strange look. It's clear she's trying to be in her element but she's a fish out of water in this place. She doesn't want to look awkward but doesn't have the experience to know what she's doing.

"Why don't we get a spot over in the corner? It's better without all the noise." It's a lie. Front and center of the room is my style. The prime place to be seen and noticed. A look of relief washes over her at my suggestion and she is quick to tell the waiter our choice.

"Why don't you indulge in a little champagne?" I ask when she orders water.

"It's a work night." She shakes her head.

"You sound like a kid saying it's a school night," I retort, looking over the menu. "How old are you? Do you have to get home in time for your curfew?"

She gives me a glance. "No, I just don't want to be sick in the morning, that's all."

"You won't be sick from one glass; no one does. If you think I'll let you get drunk, you have a surprise waiting."

"Isn't it the way with all you men? Take out a girl and get her nice and plastered so you can have your way with her?" she asks with a snide look.

"That's hardly the way for me. Do you really think I need to get a girl drunk before she lets me fuck her?" I laugh. "Come on, you should know me better than that by now."

She says nothing but the look on her face screams envy. She wants to know how many partners I've had; I can see it in her face. Except, I never kiss and tell. She'll never know the number, just as she'll never be questioned herself.

"All right, one glass of champagne," she says at last. "But I'm on to you, and if you think I'm not then you are the one with the surprise coming."

"I'll watch my step," I grin. She orders the champagne and I get a whiskey and it's not long before the conversation is flowing. She's getting relaxed and speaking freely with me. But I won't bring it up. The last thing I want to do is scare her off, and my impression is it won't take much to do that.

We'll enjoy the evening and see where it goes.

Though, the way she keeps touching my arm, I'm getting an idea where we'll end up.

12

ALEXIS

"Cut loose and have some fun." My friend's suggestion echoes in my mind as we finish our meal. What came over me to agree to have dinner with Clay? I'm still pissed at him for what he said, but then, he's trying to make up for it.

It was a gentlemanly thing to do, to say the least. He also let me pick the restaurant, and though I was as big of a bitch to opt for the most expensive one I knew, he doesn't seem to mind.

In fact, he treats me as though I was one of the social elite, though I often spend my money at thrift stores and survive on food handouts from time to time. I'm not reckless with my money; I know where it should go.

"Did you have a good time?" Clay asks as he helps me slip into my jacket. It's another courteous gesture, which takes me aback. It doesn't matter how much money one has; a gentleman should treat a lady like a lady.

But I'm still not prepared for it.

"I did, thank you," I smile warmly. It's the most genuine smile he has gotten from me and it looks like he's pleased.

"Great. Perhaps we can do it again sometime before I leave," he suggests.

"Let's not plan anything too swiftly," I reply dryly. He laughs.

We walk outside next to one another and I fight the urge to grab his hand. This isn't a date. This cannot be a date. That's too weird. I'm too familiar with someone who's going to walk out of my life in a couple of weeks. And we've only known each other for a couple of weeks anyway.

My relationships are slow-paced. Too slow at times. Men have walked out of my life because I refused to have sex with them. But my first time should be with someone special. Someone I know and trust. I'm not a wild one like Sarah. Things are safe and will stay that way.

We get into a cab and Clay smiles. "My place is closer, and you are more than welcome to come up for another drink before you go home. The tab is covered either way."

"We have to work in the morning. But thank you for the offer."

He smiles without a word and turns his attention out the window. It's a fight with myself on the entire ride to his place. Going for a few minutes, having a drink and thanking him for the night, would be polite. It won't be weird tomorrow if we do that. Right now, we should just get out of here.

He's been nothing but kind throughout the evening. Flirty, but nothing that made me feel pressured. By the time we get to his place, I give in.

"One drink, okay? I don't want to be hungover in the morning."

"You will not," he says. "I can keep an eye on how much you have."

I roll my eyes, feeling like a teenager when we step out. Clay pays the driver, then turns to me as we walk toward the shiny glass doors. "I'll call another cab when you're ready. It's not nice to leave them down here not knowing how long it'll be."

"I have money to call a cab for myself."

"No one is arguing that, but this evening was my idea, so let me cover it." We step inside the building and I'm dazed by how nice it is. The floor is so polished, it glows; there's a woman at the front desk, and people are milling about, all seemingly wealthy.

Without Clay, there would be no reason for me to be in a place like this.

He leads me straight to the elevator and the door shuts. He stands very close to me. Close enough for me to smell his affluent cologne, and arousal builds inside me. Clay is nothing like the guy I've envisioned losing my virginity to.

But for some reason, that's all right with me. He's dangerous, he's primal, he's intimidating, and he's got his sights set on me. He could have any woman in the world, but it's me he wants.

I feel on top of the world.

Though it disappoints me, he keeps his hands off me and we make our way through the hall to his penthouse. As soon as he opens the door, I'm dazed once again at the sight of everything.

"You live here?"

"Yup. What are you having?" He walks over to a full bar. This is the most beautiful place I've ever seen. He's the most incredible man I've ever met. Suddenly, I can't help myself anymore.

Sarah's words run through my mind again as I turn and slowly begin untying the back of my gown. Clay looks up from the bar. I sheepishly turn away and let the ties fall to my side. The zipper is not easy to reach but I rub my hands up and down my arms, sensing him draw closer to me.

He's directly behind me and for the first time, his skin touches mine. His hands run delicately up my arms, stopping at my neck. He gently kisses the crook of my shoulder, and then slowly unzips my dress. I turn as it falls away, revealing my bra and panties underneath. I'm ashamed I'm not wearing anything beyond what is functional, but Clay doesn't seem to care.

He presses his lips to my breasts, kissing them, sending shockwaves throughout my entire body. My lips quiver. Should I say something? Nothing comes to mind.

"Clay." My voice is trembling, but Clay isn't interested in discussion.

"Shh, just enjoy the moment," he whispers in my ear. His arousal is penetrating through his pants and it only makes me wetter. I reach back and unclip my bra as he pulls his shirt and pants off. He lays me gently down on the leather sofa, kissing me from my neck down to my panties.

I've had oral sex before, but never like Clay. His tongue runs over me with a passion. There's a delicate hunger, making me feel incredibly lustful. My legs shake and I moan, arching my back and pressing my pussy into his face. He continues to caress my body.

"You taste so good." His hot breath sends another shockwave through my body, making me tremble to his touch. My eyes are closed as he kisses his way back up my body to my neck, then pauses, his face just inches above mine. He grabs my legs and pulls me toward him, stopping only when his cock is pressed against my pussy.

We lock eyes but he says nothing as he pushes his dick into me as far as it can go. I whimper in pain but mask it to sound like pleasure. I've never felt a man inside me before and it launches my brain to a whole new level. Clay eases himself on top of me, holding me in his strong arms.

"Did I hurt you?" he asks. I shake my head, putting my hands on both sides of his face.

He leans forward, pressing his lips to mine, pumping himself inside my tight pussy. I try to concentrate on kissing him but my mind is distracted with each thrust he makes. Harder and harder, he pumps into me, and for the first time in my life, I'm overtaken with an orgasm. I cry out, clinging to him as my pussy pulses over his thick cock. He smiles as he grabs my hands, holding them above my head and pumping into me harder than before.

I've never felt a man cum. I spread my legs open wider, taking him in deeper. I can't get enough of him. I'm hooked! He thrusts a couple more times, and then his dick empties deep inside me. He pushes into me as hard as he can, holding himself as he completely pours himself into my tight pussy.

We breathe hard and I still feel some waves of orgasm, lifting myself as far as I can to kiss him tenderly once more. In the morning I'll probably wonder what I did but will worry about it when the time comes.

My virginity was given to the man I'm falling in love with, and I have no regrets.

13

CLAY

I wake up to find the opposite side of the bed slept in, but Alexis is gone. I roll onto my back and try to remember what happened. After sex, she stayed for a while and left around midnight. We moved to my bed to chat and enjoy each other's bodies again. Seems she liked me more than she let on.

She finally had to get going, and I insisted on paying for the cab. She tried to argue, but in the end, I won. I always do. She kissed me tenderly before she left. Was this a good idea?

Of course, getting a woman into my bed bears no regrets. Each time, it is a goal, and in that way, Alexis is no different than the other dozens of women. But there is something about her that is unusual, and I can't put my finger on it.

I like her, that's for sure, but before last night, she was someone I just wanted to fuck. Now that it's happened twice, I don't feel the same. Oh, I want to fuck her again, that's for sure. But that is what scares me. I've never wanted to see a woman again so soon after some sex.

Her number goes into my phone and if I get bored or can't get the lay—I'll call her. Alexis is special. Her ambition is really something. It's beautiful, and it makes me want to take her to new heights.

If she were to join my company even as an intern, no doubt it could be even better than it is now. It'll take some convincing, but hell, she was in my bed, so I can convince her to do other things.

How is it going to proceed at the mall? She was so strange after the kiss at the party, as though she regretted it, though at the time she was just as much into the moment as me. No dealing with her moodiness. If she continues being that way, I may not deal with it.

There's enough stress in my life; I don't have the time for someone who can't make up her mind. Or those who go through with something then spend the next few days in a bad mood because they wish they hadn't.

My phone rings. I sigh, roll over, and grab it off the nightstand. My eyes roll when I see it's Larry, then I check the time.

"What do you want? Do you know what time it is?"

"Good morning to you, sunshine; so glad to hear you're in your typical good mood," his cheerful self comes through the phone.

"Do you know what time it is? Most people tend to call within business hours."

"Most people aren't doing what I'm dealing with, either. If I call you during business hours, you'll make some bullshit excuse about working when you really hate that job and look forward to getting out of there as soon as possible," he rants.

"Damn, I'm glad you called me at this awful hour to tell me about my life."

"Listen, you wouldn't be getting a call if it weren't important. Are you busy?"

"Lying in bed like most people at six in the morning. What the heck are you doing?"

"Not lying in bed, which is what productive people do in the morning," he replies with a short tone. It's the first time he's so curt with me. Perhaps I'm doing a better job of getting under his skin?

"Cut the crap and tell me what the fuck you want! If this is a social call, I'm hanging up now."

"What? Is it so outlandish someone would call your moody ass this early in the morning? Be glad I keep these hours to make sure your ass is covered."

"You are more worried about covering your own ass at this point. You are more than aware the court could turn on you for not providing all the evidence in the case," I say with a yawn. "This isn't my first rodeo with lawyers or the court system."

"I don't care if you went to law school. And I'm not too worried about that anyway. The dates prove I had no idea at the time of the trial, so my ass is covered." There is a tone I can't help but respect. He's getting tired of the way I treat him, but I don't give a damn.

Lawyers are a dime a dozen, especially if they want to get paid well. I can get another one in a heartbeat. Maybe not one as good as he is, but one that will do the job.

I yawn again. "So you're calling me to tell me you have your ass covered?"

"No, I called to let you know I have some good news." His voice returns to the usual, annoyingly jovial tone.

"Well, that's a first."

"Come on, you don't mean that. I got you out of jail, didn't I?" I don't respond, so he continues, "We are going to buy the Berkshire Mall!"

That makes me sit up in bed. "What?"

"That's right. The owner, I forget his name," he starts.

"Mr. Scott?"

"Whatever, that guy. He's been steadily going under for a

while and we all hoped your little gig would stop that. It might have helped for a while, but with the amount of debt, it's not going to happen," Larry declares triumphantly.

"So what's the plan?" My heart sinks. I wonder how to go through with this. Lawyers handling it or not, they all will find out I am behind the mall's demise. I've come to enjoy their company, especially Alexis.

"Standard procedure. You're going to wait until after Christmas. The court is clear you must stay there throughout the month, but after that, we are free to do as we please," Larry says with more conquest in his tone. "I told you this would be a merry Christmas!"

"What will we do with it? Not another shopping mall." I hope to deter him.

"We'll tear the place down. What's wrong with you? We've done this a thousand times before. We'll throw something together. A casino, a car lot, who knows? But I knew you would be thrilled with the news, so just stick it out a little longer, buddy. Things are going to look up for you!" He's clearly congratulating himself on what he believes to be a success.

"Is that all?"

"Are you pleased?" he replies.

"Not overjoyed you had to do this at six in the morning. Some things really can wait."

"Well, damn, I thought I'd help you start your day well, but I see that was a mistake." His voice reverts to being annoyed.

"Yeah, leave me alone before eight." I am not backing down.

"I just wanted to let you know ..."

I hang up.

I lean back to stare at the ceiling once more, but my mind is preoccupied. We are going through with this! I hoped something would change and we could call it off but that will not happen. It's Larry's solution to the financial problem, and while he might be right, I'm not agreeing with him totally.

We've done this thousands of times before, just as he said, but never to people I care about. It's always been faces that won't haunt me at night.

How will this go over with Alexis? I'm not looking forward to that. I might very well lose her, and I want to fight against it. Except that will mean fighting against my own business and the financial problems we're facing now that I no longer engage in foreign trading.

In a single phone call, my life has become totally fucked.

14

ALEXIS

I pull on my tights and look in the mirror, not too happy to see myself. I feel weird about having sex with Clay but didn't expect this. Hundreds of emotions run through my brain, my body. Which to focus on?

My whole body is sore, but I have no regrets. It was my decision, but now I don't know what to do about Clay.

Also, there are many questions running through my head and I'm not sure how to feel about them. Does everyone wonder how they will act around the person they just had sex with? Or it is something that is perfectly normal?

Nothing seems natural or normal to me. I should learn how to handle it better. I want to talk to Clay, but at the same time, I don't want to bring it up.

Another part of me knows that's a blatant lie. The fact of the matter is I want to fuck Clay again, and I want to fuck him hard. He needs to see that I, too, can do more than just lie there and let him take me. I want to prove I can be just as erotic as he is.

But how will I do that?

How can I face him after this, and will he talk about it? Do guys talk about it? It's not something I've talked about with other girls, except when Sarah brings it up.

I sigh and put on my makeup, trying not to add more than normal. I want Clay to think I look good, and my first inclination is to put on more than usual. I want him to take me in his bedroom once more.

The ride to work is long. With ice on the roads, the vehicles move slower, but that gives me time to think about what to want tell Clay. Part of me wants to play it cool and not say a thing. Another part of me wants to tell him I had fun and hope he thinks so, too.

I step out of the cab and pay the driver, and then take a deep breath. When was the last time I was this nervous about going inside the mall? This place has become like a home to me, and I love seeing everyone.

Well, most of them. One person in particular, but I'm scared to hear what he has to say.

Squaring my shoulders, I walk into the mall, playing it cool. I don't want to draw attention, but I'm looking for Clay with every step. It's not unlike him to hide in the dressing room until the last possible second.

However, there is a slim chance he might be out already either way—I want to see him.

"Good morning, you look jolly today." Mr. Scott startles me as I walk through the door. He gives me a weird look. "A little jumpy?"

"Maybe a little. It was a long night, and it's never good if I don't sleep well."

"What were you up to?"

"Nothing." He gives me another odd look and I smile nervously. He knows me well enough to discern something is up. And definitely there is something up with me.

"I wondered if you would be here today." Clay walks up.

"Why wouldn't I be?" My heart races as Mr. Scott eyes the both of us and Clay gives me a knowing smirk. He turns to Scott, and I'm terrified he'll tell him what we did, but he chuckles instead.

"You should have heard her in the dressing room last night. So ready for a vacation and for this holiday madness to be over. She should try not showing up for once and see how good it feels." Relief floods over me so strongly, I just roll my eyes.

"You said you weren't going to say a thing about that!" I tease.

"I said you better hope I don't," he flirts back. My cheeks flush crimson and I shake my head. How has this man gotten me wrapped around his finger?

Mr. Scott eyes the two of us then shakes his head. "It's good to see you two getting along, but if either one of you dodge your shift, I'll kill both of you."

We all laugh and he shakes his head as he walks away, muttering how we'll be the death of him. I turn to Clay, suddenly feeling exposed and vulnerable. He's seen more of me than anyone else on the planet. He's touched me in ways no one else has. Could he tell I was a virgin? Or at least that I was before last night? The smirk he gives me makes me want to run and hide.

"Strange for me to beat you in to work in the morning. Was someone a little tired after last night?" My cheeks flush again.

"I might have stayed up a bit later than usual but it doesn't bother me." I toss my hair. "You should be the one who was too tired."

"I don't have much of a choice. I'll go to jail otherwise," he reminds me. "I don't think Scott would actually make good on his threat to kill you if you took a day off. You work harder than anyone else here."

"Which is why I can't take a day off," I say with another flip of my hair. Why am I doing this? It's a subtle way of flirting, and I need to stop before he gets the wrong idea.

"We better get to it," I say quickly. I turn and speedily walk to the dressing room, trying not to jog while doing it. I don't want him to know I'm falling for him. As soon as he finds out, I'll be putty in his hands.

At the same time, I want him to know I'm head over heels for him. He moved on me with such passion, such confidence—there is no doubt in my mind I am one of the greatest lays he's ever had.

At least, I would really like to think that.

15

CLAY

Since being forced into this charity business, this is the first time I am having fun. Alexis looks at me every chance she gets, and she's probably thinking about last night. I enjoyed the flirting this morning, and I want more. She's hard to figure out, but at the same time, I could probably get her to do what I want again.

She likes my confidence, and I am pretty impressed with the skill she demonstrated. She was so erotic, so tight. I don't know who she was fucking before, but they had to be someone good to teach her the skills.

I want to have her in bed again.

Except, as the day wears on, a change comes over her. She's becoming less friendly and bitchier, and she seems to lose interest in flirting with me. Something about her is putting up walls between us.

It's confusing! I want to call her out on her bullshit but am not sure how. She's younger than me, yet very mature for her age, but she and I come from two different worlds. Because of that, I can't expect her to live the same way I do, or the same way the bitches I've fucked in the past do.

By the end of our shift, she's ignoring me completely. There is something going on, but I don't care enough to find out. I've never felt this way before about anyone in my life but have no time to get caught up in some high school type of drama.

She looks scarcely old enough to be out of high school as it is! Did I make the right choice after at all?

"Hey, Scott, can I talk to you for a minute?" I ask on my way out the door. Alexis left as soon as she was able and I want to chat with him. They are close, and he might have some inside information to share.

Not much, just enough to learn what's going on with her.

"Don't tell me you're quitting, are you?" Mr. Scott has a concerned look in his eyes. I shake my head.

"No, but I wanted to ask you about Alexis. Did she seem out of the ordinary to you today?" I don't care what he thinks about my relationship with her.

"What do you mean?" he asks. "Did she seem sick? Is there anything I can do?"

"No, it's nothing like that. She didn't seem as happy as she usually is. I mean, she was fine this morning, but there definitely seemed to be something wrong by the time she left." He's the kind of man to see how she's doing, and I don't want her to know that.

"You know, as long as I've known Alexis, which is a pretty long time by now, she goes through these moods. At times she's in high spirits, then there are times she's withdrawn and sullen. You never really know what you get with her, which is partially what makes her interesting," Scott laughs.

"How long do these things last? Not that I'm stalking her."

"No, of course not. The two of you are becoming friends, and that's great. She needs more support in her life." His face darkens. I give him an inquisitive look, not sure how to proceed.

What is he talking about? "I shouldn't trouble you with her past, but let's just say there's been some hardship."

"Her sister ... I still feel bad about the charity when I first got here," I say with a sigh.

"It's not only that. Her sister was just the beginning of her troubles. The death of a child is tough for any parent. It was the death of them. I mean figuratively. A family devastated in several ways has taken its toll on her." Scott shakes his head again.

Sighing, I wish I knew what to say. but am uncertain of how to bring it up without prying. After all, I'm the one who will leave in the next couple weeks, and all of this will be torn down.

It won't surprise me if she hates me for it, and that in itself keeps me at bay.

"You shouldn't be bombarded with all of this information. We all have our own paths, and she was given a shitty one," Scott sighs, and then chuckles. "The fact that you hate this time of year has been broached more than once. That stems from extreme pain."

"It's the charity work. People are more caring and giving this time of year, so she's able to see growth in her work," Scott explains. He tucks his notebook under his arm and checks his phone.

"I don't mean to run off but I need to make this next meeting. There might be a chance we can stave off the big corporations after all. Fingers crossed," Mr. Scott grins hopefully. Another stab of pain runs through my chest. He doesn't know my corporation will buy him out and the fact that he hopes to stop it makes me feel worse.

"Good luck with that," I smile and pat him on the arm. "With the miracle of the season, you can find something."

He gives me a strange look.

"What's that glance for?"

"You said the miracle of the season, as though you believe in such things." He shakes his head.

"Is that bizarre?" I'm feeling defensive, but wish not to let it show. I've been nothing but difficult since my arrival at the mall but need to admit, being here every day has helped me see things in a different perspective.

What he does might not be the best, or even what Alexis does, but the holiday season seems better and I want to be nicer about it.

"It's funny. That suit is rubbing off on you." Scott laughs and shakes his head. "I'm glad!"

"I'll be glad when this mess is over." I sigh and shake my head. "I'm sick of doing this, and can admit it."

"You'll be glad when it's done, but you'll miss us when you go back to your fancy life," Scott comments with another laugh. "Anyway, it will not look good if I miss this meeting. Take care."

"You too. Oh, and Scott?" I stop. His eyebrows rise. "You won't say a thing about this to Alexis, will you?"

"Not a word. She likes you, but will not get her hopes up." He smiles once more. What does he mean by that? I stop myself. He's just teasing. Scott always teases everyone around him.

What did he mean by getting her hopes up? Did she say something?

Is there a chance after all?

16

ALEXIS

Quickly, I walk out to the cab that's waiting for me outside. What came over me? I had to get out of there as soon as possible. Clay should not get the wrong idea, and I have no clue how to do it.

A huge part of me wants to have a relationship with him, but the more rational side knows that will never happen. He is way out of my league and our fucking might not have been an expression of love so much as him simply wishing to get laid.

There are too many alarms signal to let myself fall for him. I need to get away from this.

My phone chimes. It's a number I don't recognize. I open the text, curious.

Hey, Alexis, it's Clay. We did not have a chance to chat today, so I wondered if you would like to grab a cup of coffee to sort things out?

I wait for a minute, looking at the text.

How did you get my number?

The reply comes immediately.

Sandy gave it to me. What do you say?

I roll my eyes. Of course Sandy would feel free to hand out

my number without my permission. Mr. Scott wouldn't do that. He knows too well that I get pissed when that happens. More people should respect that—so much gossip going on at the mall! Everyone feels free to hand out everyone else's information.

We can, but I don't have a lot of time. I hit send before thinking about it further. A part of me wants to meet up with him and another part wants to avoid the entire situation.

That's fine. Let's meet at Gregory's Diner, if you don't mind. Great coffee. Are you free?

Again, I hesitate. He's waiting for an answer, but I am not able to send one. Finally, I say fuck it.

All right, I'll be there. But again, I don't have a lot of time.

The driver gets the new directions and turns that way. I settle into the seat and sigh. He'll want to talk about last night. At least, I'm quite sure. What will I say? I can't tell him the truth. If he finds out he was my first and how I feel about him, he'll dismiss me as any other woman who lost their v card.

Yet, if I lie to him, I'll only cheat myself out of what could possibly be a good relationship. Stranger things have happened, and it wouldn't surprise me if that is what happens with us.

At least, a girl can only hope.

We pull up in front of the diner and I pay the cab, stepping out of the car. It's a busy place, but it won't be difficult to find him. Few people in the world look so elegant in a suit, and he always wears one.

At least, when he's not Santa Claus.

I step inside and scan the room for a familiar face. Clay is sitting at the breakfast bar with his back to me. It's something I really like about the diner. I immediately plan what to order. Then I've got the impulse to walk up behind him.

It will be immature but funny. The closer I get to him, the more I consider doing it. He's on the phone with someone. That will make it even funnier. I'm determined not to get his attention until I'm able to scare him.

Other people in the diner look my way, but they seem amused at what is about to happen. None of them blow my cover.

"Listen, Larry, make sure this is flawless," Clay says into the phone. I don't know who Larry is, but Clay certainly talks to him a lot.

"No, that's not a good way to do things. No, I'm not getting soft. We have one chance, and I don't want to blow it like the last one. I talked to the owner of the building yesterday. Yes, Scott. He said he's on his way to a meeting that can keep the business from going under. Is that true?" Clay speaks in a low voice but I am standing close enough to hear every word.

My heart sinks into my stomach, racing at the same time. The potential of the business going under was clear, but Clay never mentioned he had something to do with it. In fact, he always acted like he was just as surprised as the rest of us.

Taking a deep breath, I wait to hear more before drawing conclusions.

"Listen, if we are going to strike this deal, we have to do it right. I'm not getting into more trouble or work like this again. I'm above this, and intend to stay that way," Clay declares. It's all I have to hear.

A noise escapes my throat. It's partly a sob, and somewhat a gasp, but enough to get Clay's attention. He turns around, surprised, then quickly wraps up the call.

"Look, Larry, we'll talk about this later. No, I don't care what you have to say about it, we'll talk about it later!" He hangs up while the other man is still talking. He looks at me with astonishment.

"I didn't think you would be here so soon. I would have saved that phone call," he says with a grim face. He's trying to be suave but I can see right through it. He knows he's been caught.

"What the fuck was that? Do you really think you will be able to get away with this?"

"It's not what you think." He rises from his chair and puts his hand on my shoulder.

"Don't touch me! You are a liar! I want nothing to do with you!" I fight to keep my voice down but it's too late. Customers are already looking at us yet trying to mind their own business.

"You don't know what you heard!" Clay snaps back. He has a temper. It's one of the news stories. But I'm not going to sit here and listen to him gas-lighting me, knowing what has been said.

"Does Scott know about this?"

"No, and I would appreciate if you didn't say anything. Again, you don't know what you heard just now, and I won't fight with you right here in the middle of the diner," Clay speaks in a calmer tone.

"Well, you don't have to worry about fights with me because I never want to see you again!" I want to sound angrier than I am but all that comes out are tears and sobs. Everyone is staring at us now and I can't take it anymore.

I turn on my heel and walk out the door, ignoring Clay's calls to come back.

I know what he said, and he can fuck off.

∽

One Week Later

17

CLAY

"I don't understand. It's not at all like Alexis to ditch her obligations. What could have upset her so much?" Mr. Scott shakes his head. "I thought the two of you got along."

"The last time I spoke to you before talking to her was when you said she got into these moods."

"Yeah. There's a difference between someone getting in a mood and simply dropping out of life." Mr. Scott shakes his head. "She's done this sort of thing to an extent, but she's never done it like this. Whatever happened must have really upset her."

"She heard part of my conversation on the phone and she misunderstood what's going on," I say, exasperated. I've already told him several times, yet he keeps pressing me. He's trying to find out what was said, but I can't tell him. Not until I have more details.

"What did she hear? I'm not asking you to tell me the entire conversation, but what could she possibly have heard that got her so riled up?" he presses.

"It was a private conversation, and she eavesdropped. She

could have been more mature about it and talked to me instead of running off. It's not fair to either of us." I let the anger show in my voice. I don't care what he thinks.

"It's certainly not fair to the company. I was depending on her finishing with the holiday. Without her, I doubt we'll be able to pull in the crowd we have," he sighs.

"The main attraction is Santa, so where is the problem?" I know I'm being snarky, but he's only fighting to find out more of my story.

"It's a team effort. You bring in the people; she gets them to you. It doesn't matter if we've got a thousand folks standing in line if total chaos is around us," Mr. Scott says rather sharply. It's rare for him to get that way, but after stumbling through the week getting help from the other staff, he's at his wit's end.

It's only a few more days until Christmas, and then all of this will go down. We are entering the biggest days of the year, and he wants to push as much as he can to increase the sales.

"Look, at the end of the day, it was up to her to leave. You can't push that on me any longer," I remark, still harsh.

I act like I don't care anymore, but the fact of the matter is the opposite—I care a lot. I have been trying to get a hold of Alexis since she ran out of the diner. She does not answer her phone or text messages. I would stop by and talk to her but haven't the slightest idea where she lives.

The only times we hung out outside of work were the night she came home with me, and the meeting we had at the diner. I really don't know much about this woman.

"Sounds like the tides have really turned. It appeared the two of you were starting to like each other," Mr. Scott comments.

"What the fuck could have given you that idea?" I don't want to talk about it anymore, and he's still fishing for the details.

"I'll never understand love, to be honest." He shakes his head.

"Why are you talking about, love? I'm not in love with her!" I don't want to shout. The last thing I want is for anyone else to hear this. The gossip that goes on ... I don't want to make the situation even worse.

"Man, the way you look at her. It's in your face when you stop for a moment, a child on your lap, and watch what she's doing. Oh, don't look at me like that. I'm not saying it's a blatant look, but it didn't escape me. I doubt it escaped her, either." There's a twinkle in his eye.

"I can hardly blame you. I've been in love with that girl since the day she walked into this mall, looking for help with her charity." He shakes his head with a wistful look in his eyes. It stings to think about Alexis' charity and how she will not have a place to set it up.

She had a lot of plans. She told me more than once how important it was to her and I supported her every step of the way. At least, I wanted to. I hope she understands one day that I'm not entirely in charge of my firm or the decisions they make.

She seems to think I'm the king of the world and able to call the shots with everyone who walks through my door, though I'm really at the mercy of many others.

How could she know that? She was a startup with some visions but not the power to make it happen. It was part of the reason I fell in love with her. I love that ambition! And the drive. She's not the type to get discouraged with the shit around her.

That is, when she's not hurt by the person she loves.

"Your sentiment is appreciated, but you have it all wrong. Alexis does not want to see me again. She's made that much clear."

Mr. Scott sighs. He wants to comfort me and tell me she's just angry and will come around. He believes in holiday miracles—complete bullshit to me! Even with the magic of the season, there is a way everything may just not be all right.

He can't see into the future! He agreed she's never done this before. He's figuring out what's going on! But just like me, he has no idea. Still, Alexis hasn't come to tell him what she heard.

It's admirable she has not.

"She'll come around eventually, and your life will go back to normal. You'll pull through with this business, and she'll have her charity, and who knows? One day the two of you might fall in love." I weakly suggest.

"Oh no! Your hope in the matter is appreciated but I am too old for her. She'll never turn a second glance to a man my age," he chuckles. "I need someone like her but more like me. Age wise, that is."

"And one day you will," I grab my beard and grapple it over my head. "Break time is over and I better get back out there to relieve Brittany."

"That girl needs all the help she can get, that's for sure," Scott laughs. "You should have seen the look on her face when I told her she'd be the elf today."

I laugh but my heart isn't in it. I miss Alexis, and wish there was a way to get a hold of her. Neither one of us wishes to involve Scott. It looks like he's the only hope to reconnect with her. I feel bad about what happened and admittedly, she wasn't wrong in her assumptions.

She doesn't know I'm also doing my best to fight this. I will do anything to make sure the Berkshire Mall stays in business.

I pause on my way out the door.

Maybe it will mean the worst.

18

ALEXIS

I look at my phone and sigh. I'm in the middle of helping with dinner at a local homeless shelter. No time for harassing calls from Clay or Mr. Scott. Mr. Scott is simply worried and wondering where I ended up, but Clay is just trying to talk again.

And that'll never happen.

I'm hurt beyond words. I never talk about my charity because that will destroy the idea before it becomes a reality. Clay gave me the impression he was different.

Sure, at first he seemed like the kind of guy who didn't care about anyone but himself when he had all those kids on his lap. But the more we got to know each other, the more I perceived him in a different light. There was even a part of me that didn't believe that he did the crimes he was accused of.

"Pay attention to what you're doing, please?" Greg, my boss, pushes past with his arms loaded down with plates of food.

"Sorry."

"Phones are off limits during shifts," he grumbles.

"Sorry." I slip it into my pocket and tend to the plates of food in front of me. My job is to portion out the dinner and place the plates on the tray, but it's difficult sometimes. We have to keep the portions decent, but as hungry as some of the people in the room are, they should get a little extra.

I have no control over who gets which plate, so I need to stick to the rules.

My phone chimes again. I glance over my shoulder. Greg is in the other room handing out the plates. He'll move as quick as he can, but it gives me some time to check the message. It's from Scott. A part of me wants to tell him to leave me alone, then another part can't.

I glance back to Greg before opening the text.

Can you please stop by the mall later today? I really want to talk to you.

I send a hurried reply, knowing that my phone has to be put away quickly.

I'm sorry, Mr. Scott, but I can't bring myself to it.

I go back to serving the plates. My phone chimes once more. It's him again.

I've been nothing but good to you. You at least should give me an explanation.

My heart sinks as I slip the phone back into my pocket. He's right. He has done more for me throughout the years than anyone else. I can't just leave him high and dry. No matter how angry I am with anyone, at least I should face my boss.

I text saying I'll be there but also that I can't be on my phone at the moment.

Now it's time to watch the clock.

I ARRIVE at the mall still wearing my work clothes. I don't care if bits of stuffing and gravy are splattered on the front. I take pride in my contribution in the community, and won't stop for anyone.

My heart pounds trying to decide what I'll tell Mr. Scott. He deserves to know the truth but I don't want to betray Clay. There's a part of me that's filled with compassion for him, and I don't want to cause more trouble.

If Mr. Scott were to find out, there is little doubt in my mind that Clay would be fired. He is so close to finishing his sentence; I don't want to be the one to send him to jail, no matter what he did to me. As long as I don't see him, as long as I just talk to Mr. Scott, I'll be okay.

He's in his office.

"There you are! Please sit down," he says warmly. I obey, but it gives me an uncomfortable feeling.

"How are you?"

"Fine," I reply.

"You left really suddenly," he presses. "There has to be a reason for it. I thought you would stay beyond the holidays and get your charity set up."

"I thought so at the time, but you know, things change," I say grimly.

"But what changed? There has to be something. I know you well enough. No way you would have just ditched me like that." There's pain in his voice, but I can't find the words.

"It wasn't you or anything you did, trust me," I swallow hard, mincing my words. "It's just that I learned some new information that wasn't very good, so I decided to leave."

"What information is that?"

"I'm not at liberty to say."

"Maybe it would be easier explain if I brought Clay into the room. He's just as confused as me about what happened, and the two of you can work it out," he says cheerfully.

"No, don't do that!" I hold my arm out toward the door. Mr. Scott doesn't listen. He pulls the door open and Clay walks in. Immediately, I'm filled with fury once more. I don't want to see

Clay! I'm pissed at them both for putting me in this predicament.

"Hey," Clay blurts out. I look down and refuse to answer.

"It's obvious you don't want to talk to me, but there are a few things we need to discuss," he presses.

"Yes, the two of you sit and talk it out. I'm here to mediate. This way we get all the answers, clear up misunderstandings, and leave the office happy," Mr. Scott says cheerfully as he sits down.

"You are an idiot if you think I'll sit here and be the bad guy!" I shout. "You are the one who is ruining everything, not me!"

"What are you talking about?" Mr. Scott asks. Clay is growing uneasy and I have to choose my words carefully. I still don't want to betray him, but it's more tempting with each passing moment.

"You misheard some issues you are not supposed to be a part of, and you overreacted," Clay says after clearing his throat.

"I heard you on the phone! What you said was as clear as what I hear right now. Don't you dare tell me any different!" My voice is low and my tone even.

"You eavesdropped on something and you're trying to use it against me," Clay declared.

"Why the heck would I do that?" I laugh. "What would that prove?"

"I don't know. You are the one doing it!" Clay snaps.

"I'm only coming clean—exposing you to be a liar, and ruining the picture of the angel in disguise everyone thought you were!" I lower my arms to my sides as I shout. I don't care if anyone in the halls hears this. I am pissed, and will let the world know.

"Okay, you both need to back up on this," Mr. Scott interjects once more. "What are you talking about?"

"Clay here plans on selling our business out from under us,

just like the greedy corporate he is!" I snap. "He doesn't give a damn about what happens to you, me, or any of us!"

"Easy, easy!" Mr. Scott soothes. "Take a deep breath and sit down. Let's get to the bottom of this."

"Ask him! You'll be right at the bottom of this," I say defiantly. "Since you insisted he come in, why not ask him yourself?"

"Clay is right. You misunderstood what's going on and you aren't thinking about it clearly," Mr. Scott announced.

"What the fuck are you talking about?" I turn on him. "Men like him know what they're doing!"

"I can't put him on the spot with legal matters as such, but there is no such thing happening," Mr. Scott says with anger in his voice. It's rare for him to be infuriated with me but it happens. Why is he angry now? It's only making me feel worse.

This is happening right under his nose, and he doesn't realize.

"If you are going to be so naïve to think he's incapable of doing something like that, then you haven't paid much attention to the papers." I gain a new sense of defiance.

"His past is none of your business," Mr. Scott says. Clay sits quietly throughout the whole thing, and I try to read the look on his face—without much success.

"I won't be here to watch all this fade away. You can have me, or you can have Clay. We both know who you'll pick." I flip my hair. Mr. Scott looks at me as if thinking I've lost my mind, but I've actually made it up.

I will not work for a business that's going under, and not for a man who doesn't believe me. Or one who is slowly stealing my life's dream away. Mr. Scott can figure it out in the end, but I won't be there when he does.

"Good day to you both." I nod my head. Mr. Scott still looks confused, and Clay appears dismayed I'm going through with the threat. He knows Mr. Scott and I have been friends for a long time, but I'll prove to them both that I will not work in a place I don't believe in.

I turn on my heel and walk out the door, slamming it closed behind me. I don't want to hear Mr. Scott asking me to reconsider, or even to come back and talk to them. I've said my piece, and they've made their stance clear.

Clay can have the mall. I've worked hard without it, and though it's another closed door, I'm determined to recover.

Somehow, some way, I'll make this charity happen.

19

CLAY

The rest of my day is spent trying to make the kids happy, but having a terrible time of it. It's tough being a jolly Santa Claus when my world has crashed down around me. I'm torn. She was so upset in the office—it showed in her face.

More than likely I'll never see her again, and that breaks my heart to a big extent. I have never fallen for a woman like this before. Sure, there have been ones I've wanted to fuck multiple times, but never have I felt I met the woman I could spend the rest of my life with.

Knowing I had that chance and now she's gone is more than I can stand. She had a dream of building that charity here in the mall. She cares a lot for Mr. Scott and the others who work here. She doesn't want to see all of it go away.

She's obviously aggravated with him so he can see the truth. It hurts me that I didn't stand up for her when she needed me to. I stayed silent and let her look like a fool in front of one of her best friends. I feel sorry for her.

I need to make it right with her. What will that take? The

only way is to get her back here—and to save this place. It won't be easy. I'll have to do something I don't want to do.

"Next!" I'm working with Brittany again and she isn't sure how to handle the size of the crowd. She's trying, but she's rather overwhelmed. However, it's Christmas Eve, and this is the last chance these kids will get to see Santa Claus.

The next child hurries over and crawls up onto my lap. He looks at me nervously with his big eyes.

"Hello, young man! And what would you like for Christmas?" I hope the parents get all these kids what they want. Even though I'm not the real Santa, even though there isn't a real Santa, I hope each of these kids will believe in him by the end of tomorrow night.

It's something that makes Alexis special and one of the things I don't want to lose in the coming year. How many things about me will change because of her? I am quick to make changes for her.

"Santa?" the boy asks before he crawls off my lap.

"What is it, young man?" It's so formal to talk like this, but I don't have a choice. There are rules that have to go along with the mall, and I have to follow them even if I want to be friendlier with him.

"What do you want for Christmas?" He looks at me with his wide brown eyes. None of the other children have ever asked me that. Most of them were too scared to do more than whisper what they wanted, then sit and stare at the camera while their enthusiastic parents had their photo taken.

"Do you know what you want?" he presses.

"Santa, we need to keep this going," Brittany coaxes. She doesn't want to end the moment but she, too, has rules to follow. It's her job to keep the line going. This is the busiest we've been since the start, and I'm a little overwhelmed myself.

"You know what I want?" I know this needs to be wrapped up.

He shakes his head.

"I want to spend it with my family."

His eyes grow wider than before, and he smiles. "That's what I want too."

He hops off my lap and I smiled as he trots down the aisle back to his parents. His mother holds a baby in her arms, a child too small to know what the holiday is yet. It's a happy family, and he meant what he said.

What is it he wanted before his question? I really hope he gets it. Somehow, he reminds me of Alexis, and I feel more resolved than ever to continue with this plan.

At the end of the shift, my heart races walking back to Mr. Scott's office. We haven't spoken much throughout the day, not since Alexis came to his office. I have to speak with him, and he needs to know the truth.

"Can I bother you for a moment?" I knock on his open door. He looks at me in surprise.

"Yes, please come in. I wanted to talk to you too."

"You first." He won't be able to think clearly once he hears what I tell him.

"I wanted to apologize for what happened earlier. Alexis is not in her right mind at times and often assumes the worst." He nods toward the uniform on the table.

"No, let me speak," I interrupt. "There was actually a lot more to what she said than I let on."

His eyebrows rise. "The only way she'll come back to this mall is when I make things right, so I'll be upfront. I'm removing myself from the volunteer position, and I want you to accept this check."

"What? You only have two days left! You'll end up in jail!" Scott confides with alarm in his voice.

"Just read the letter in there; it'll explain everything. For once in my life, I need to do the right thing by everyone else's standards. I can't go through life being such an egotist. I have to do more than that."

He looks at me, dumbstruck, as I turn to walk out of the office. He picks up the letter from the desk, so I turn. "Give me a few minutes. I don't want to be here when the cops show up. That would be too traumatizing for the kids."

His mouth falls open, and he wants to think of something to say, but he's so shocked he doesn't know where to even begin.

I, on the other hand, don't want to hear from him. I want to get out of here and have a couple more drinks before spending Christmas behind bars. Somehow, it'll be better than I thought. There's no more of the shame and fear I felt before.

I finally feel like I did the right thing, and I'm at peace with my decision.

Even if it does mean I'll get locked up.

20

ALEXIS

"I said I'm at the homeless shelter." I have an annoyed tone to my voice. I don't want to talk to Scott anyway, but once again he is relentless until I answer.

"You've got to hear this." There's excitement in his voice, and I sigh.

"All right, but I've got to get back inside. They can fire volunteers, and I don't want that on my résumé." I sound exasperated, but after the way he treated me, I don't care. I am not going to treat him with the same respect when he basically called me a liar.

"First of all, I'm sorry," he starts.

I sigh. "Is that all?"

"No, there's something else, and you're going to be shocked when you hear what it is." Once again, the exhilaration is in his voice.

"Come on, tell me."

"Okay, here goes."

My heart races as I arrive outside the door to Clay's penthouse. It isn't the best idea to show up unannounced but I need to see him. I ring the bell and wait, my heart still racing.

He opens the door a few seconds later and is surprised to see me.

"Hey," he says

"They dropped the charges!" I smile. A confused look grows on his face.

"What?"

"The bank. When they heard about the donation and what you did for the mall, they dropped all the charges! You're a free man!" Before he has a chance to respond, I throw myself onto him. Our mouths meet, and I start kissing him. Not long ago, I was still a virgin, but I've known how to kiss for a while.

I slip my tongue inside his mouth. He moans, picks me up, and carries me to his bed. We are already breathing hard as he yanks off my jacket, then the dress I am wearing underneath. My hands are at his clothes, pulling at the T-shirt, then working on the jeans.

He helps me get them off, then crawls over me on the bed. Our mouths meet. He's on top of me, his body pressed against mine, his hands exploring me with as much passion as his tongue. I groan and writhe on the sheets beneath him, spreading my legs and pressing my hips to his hard cock, begging him to enter me.

Clay doesn't wait long. He takes his dick in his hand and presses it to the lips of my tight pussy, sliding himself into me. I cry out in pain, but not with the same intensity as before. I love taking his full length inside me.

He thrusts himself into me while I grind my hips onto him. We have the same rhythm—him on top working on me while I clutch him with both my arms. I press his body to mine, putting my hand on his ass and pulling him into me.

His cock is sliding in circles within me, touching me right where I need to be touched, feeling me all over. Each new move sends me closer and closer to a climax, and a scream is building inside me.

"Cum for me, baby," he says with a passion. "I need you to cum."

The orgasm overtakes me, sending waves of passion and pleasure throughout my entire body. Nearly at the exact same time, his cock buckles and throbs inside me, moving as he fills me with his load. I moan and hold him as he cums, enjoying the moment.

When our orgasms subside, he looks into my eyes, brushing the hair out of my face.

"I can't believe you're here."

"I can't believe what you did for me. For us," I whisper. "Thank you."

"I am proud to support someone who believes in something. Grow that charity and start saving lives. I believe in you."

His lips meet mine, and we share a long, passionate kiss, our bodies still pressed against each other, moving as one. He is slowly getting soft inside me, but I don't want him to go. I've never felt so attached to anyone and wish the moment could last forever.

"There is one problem, however," he says.

"What's that?"

"What about you and me?"

I look at surprised. "What do you mean, you and me?"

"You are the first woman who has taken my heart, and I don't want this to end. Of course, I need to go back to my life as a CEO, but I can still make the time to come down to the mall every once in a while. I would love to see how your charity grows," he says in a low tone.

"Are you asking me to be your girlfriend?" I let the shock show in my voice.

"Do you want a boyfriend for Christmas?" Clay asks with a teasing smile. My heart skips a beat. I never thought he would ever consider that. I wondered if fucking him again would be a good idea, but had to think of some way to show my gratitude.

Knowing he wants to be more than friends is a complete shock, and I can't do anything but snuggle into his chest.

"Is that a yes?" He laughs, rolling off of me, and I snuggle against him once more. The snow is falling lightly outside the window and a ray of sunshine fills the room.

"That is a definite yes," I say at last. He leans forward and kisses my forehead, caressing my arm. I lost my family years ago to tragedy, and wanted to devote the rest of my life to serving others in need. Not once have I thought I would find a man like Clay, and it's great I did.

"I think we should go out," Clay says.

"Are you sure?" I ask reluctantly.

"I do." His smile makes my heart flutter. "I want to take my new girlfriend out for some Christmas fun."

Slowly, a smile spreads across my face as he gets out of bed.

"What do you say?" He looks at me. He extends his hand. I take it, looking up into his eyes.

"I'll grab my jacket."

THE END.

SIGN UP TO RECEIVE FREE BOOKS

Sign Up to Receive Free E-Books and Audiobook Codes.

Would you like to read **The Unexpected Nanny, Dirty Little Virgin** and **other romance books** for free?

You can sign up to receive these free e-books and audiobooks by typing this link into your browser:

https://www.steamyromance.info/free-books-and-audiobooks-hot-and-steamy/

Or this one:

https://www.steamyromance.info/the-unexpected-nanny-free/

PREVIEW OF HER DARK SECRET
A BILLIONAIRE & A VIRGIN ROMANCE

By Michelle Love

CHAPTER ONE

Attico Fibonacci gazed out of the window of the jet as it crossed from France into Switzerland. Geneva lay below him, the Alps looming large as the jet circled and came down to land. He felt a slight tightness in his chest as he considered where he was going —his alma mater, the school he had left nearly twenty years ago, *L'Académie Amérique du Genève*.

As the plane landed, he pushed the thought of returning away and concentrated on why he was here—to give the commencement speech.

At almost forty, Attico Fibonacci could easily be called the most successful alumnus of the school, with the possible exception of his older brother, Tony. Both brothers had graduated with highest honors, fifteen years apart, and were the pride of their school. Tony, traveling to Geneva with his younger brother, had only good memories of the school. Attico, less so. Yes, he had been the 'it' boy, but then if his fellow students had known what had happened there …

"Stop thinking about it," Tony said now, interrupting Attico's reverie. "It wasn't your fault, Atti, and it was over twenty years ago. Stop dwelling."

Attico nodded but said nothing. Easier said than done when you knew you'd ruined somebody's life. As if on cue, his cell phone buzzed. Lucinda, his now *ex*-girlfriend. "Hey, Lu."

"Hey, Atti." Thank God their split had been amicable—at least on the surface. "I just wanted to let you know that my lawyer has sent over the papers for the settlement."

"Good. I'll get them signed and back to you as soon as I get back to New York." He hesitated. "How are you?"

"I'm good," Lucinda said lightly and then there was an awkward pause. It might be amicable but it was still painful. "Bucky's missing you."

Their dog was an oversized German Shepherd, Bucky, of whom they shared custody. "Just Bucky?" Attico said softly and heard Lucinda sigh.

"Don't, Atti. Don't make this harder."

"I'm sorry. I miss you."

"I miss you too, baby, I do, but we both know this was for the best." Lucinda's voice was kind but firm. "You will always, *always* be my best friend."

"Right back at you, Lulu."

She chuckled but there was sadness in her voice. "I'll see you soon, Atti."

"Bye."

God, it still hurt. Lucinda had broken up with him almost a year ago after a six-year relationship. Attico had known, in his heart, that she was unhappy, that their relationship had turned to platonic friendship years before, but he had stuck his head in the sand until it became painfully clear that it was over.

He hadn't been able to see how he could ever love someone else after Lucinda. Grateful for the opportunity to leave New York for a few days, now as he got into the town car which would take them back to the Academy, he wondered if running away had been the best idea.

Chapter One

Beside him in the car, Tony gave a sigh. "Dude, I hope you perk up during this trip. You've been on a downer for months now. Attico, you're rich, single, and handsome. Live a little."

And he was right. Attico Fibonacci often appeared at the top of the "Most Eligible Bachelor" lists in the high-society magazines. A self-made billionaire in the property world, he was a gloriously good-looking man, tall, broad, bright green eyes, and dark, wild curls. Tony, older by fifteen years, was a dapper man with a shaved head, dark brown eyes, and an air of elegance whereas Attico was considered beautiful by both his peers and the women who flocked to him, his face both boyish and mesmerizing. He wore a light beard to make his face look his age, but even he knew the effect his looks had on both men and women. He wore a suit well, but he was more at home in blue jeans and a vintage tee.

Looking at the Fibonacci boys, no one would never guess they were brothers. Attico looked exactly like his father, Sebastiano, an Oliver Reed-lookalike with an air of wild menace and beauty. Tony took after their late mother, the serene and delicate Giovanna. But the brothers, despite their age difference, were devoted to each other. Tony was a confirmed bachelor, a lover of both men and women, who played the field, even now when he was in his mid-fifties. He could get away with it, his natural charm and extrovert tendencies making every transgression forgiven.

Attico, on the other hand, was surprisingly shy. He was a homeboy, preferring to spend time reading or walking the dog or watching television with someone. He eschewed parties, and that was one of the reasons he was now regretting agreeing to speak at his alma mater's commencement. There would be a reception afterward, and he was already dreading it, making nonsensical small talk with people he didn't know. God.

He must have given a sigh because he heard Tony make an

irritated noise. "Atti, stop being a downer. Look at this place; it's paradise. After the hoo-ha is over, we're going out on the town and you're going to get laid, comprendé?"

"Whatever." Attico was aware he sounded like a sulky teenager and gave an apologetic smile. He didn't want to bring Tony down. "Sure, bro. Let's do it."

"That's more like it."

Attico smiled at his brother then, as the car turned a corner, he saw it. L'Académie Amérique, standing on the shores of Lake Geneva, a vast Belle époque chateau, home to the richest of the rich, less than two hundred of the world's most privileged students.

The setting for Attico's worst nightmare.

CHAPTER TWO

Temple Dubois wiped her brother's mouth and smiled at him. "All clean and tidy, Luc."

He smiled at her, his brown eyes alert and twinkling, but Temple knew he only saw her smile, not who she really was to him. The accident had made it impossible for Luc, and for almost twenty years, she had been the "lady that smiled" to him.

Not his sister. Not his caregiver. But "the lady with the smile." Temple could live with that. The doctors and nurses had told her that, for Luc, for him to be able to describe anyone like that was a miracle. The accident had stripped him of almost everything else—his ability to walk, to reason, and had robbed him of almost all of his speech.

"He might not remember you're his sister, his blood," the kindly doctor had told her a long time ago, "but somewhere in there, he knows and acknowledges that you are special to him."

Temple smiled at her brother now. The one thing the accident hadn't taken was his beauty, his sweet soul. Though he was older than her by almost twelve years, Temple now felt like the older sibling, having looked after him since she was eight years old, almost entirely by herself, with support from the Academy.

Now, as she kissed Luc goodbye and set off back to the Academy, she let out a deep breath. She had a week to herself after commencement before the summer school began and she intended to do ... nothing. She relished the thought of being alone in her tiny apartment in Geneva, the home she had finally been able to afford after years of living at the Academy, paying her way by teaching, and now she couldn't wait to escape to her own little haven.

She had a stack of books, plenty of good food and great music, and she intended to hole up and ignore the phone and all other humans—except for her daily visit to Luc, of course.

When she got back to the school, she went to her office, unlocking it, and she hadn't been back for more than five minutes when there was a knock and one of her students stuck her head around the door.

Temple smiled at her. "Hey, Zella, come in. What can I do for you?"

Zella, a gorgeous teenager with long dark hair and a thousand-watt smile, sat down opposite her. "A favor, and I know it's a long shot, but do you have a spare spot in your class for the summer?"

Temple's eyebrows shot up. "You're not going home?"

Zella rolled her eyes. "Mum's decided she's going to marry The Swede and their honeymoon is apparently a six-month long affair, so ... She said I could stay home alone, but honestly, I'd rather be here. Olivia, Barry and Rosario are staying. So ... any chance?"

Temple smiled at her. "I'm sure I can squeeze you in, but you know it's going to be pretty intensive, right? The exhibition we're studying is only going to be at the school for a couple of weeks, so we have field trips planned almost every day and classes afterward. Long days ... can you cope?"

"Pah, of course. It's going to be cool, right? First time the museum has allowed these items out to loan?"

The museum she was talking about was a small but prestigious museum specializing in Wiccan and occult artifacts and Temple was leading a special course for history geeks, as she called them. She nodded now. "Right. But you know that some of the items we're being loaned actually belonged to the school first?"

Zella nodded. "I heard. You know which ones?"

Temple grinned. "Spoilers."

"Aww, Temple ..."

Temple never stood on formality. She was Temple or Tem to both her colleagues and her students. It was one of the reasons she was so popular. "Nope, sorry, kiddo. All will be revealed in a week's time. Now, look, you've cleared staying with Facilities, right?"

"They told me I needed to confirm a place on the course first."

Temple scribbled out a note and signed it. "Here you go." She smiled at her student. Zella was one of *those* kids—bright, curious, smart, and collaborative. And kind, which was more of an issue than Temple ever expected when she started teaching. "Take that to Facilities and if they have any questions, get them to call me."

"Thanks, Temple, I appreciate it."

"Looking forward to commencement?"

Zella rolled her eyes. "It sounds like fun but I know it's going to be three minutes of excitement, and two hours of boredom."

"Yup, pretty much. See you later."

Temple closed up her office about 6:00 p.m. and walked through the halls to the refectory. Most of the students were in there and she grabbed some hot food and sat down with a bunch of them, chatting easily, trying to fend off questions about the exhibition from the lucky few who had enrolled in her class. If she had been honest with Zella earlier, she would have told her that the class had been full for weeks ... but it was *Zella*, and for summer school, Temple didn't mind playing favorites.

Someone nudged her on the back, then sat down by her. Nicolai Lamont, the school's professor of languages, and her best friend, grinned at her. "Hey babe."

Temple laughed. As always, his attempts at American slang in his thick French accent made her giggle—he did it on purpose now. "Hey, y'all."

Nicolai was her very best friend at the school—and Temple had always had a little crush on him, even if that crush was futile. Nicolai was very happily married to Rainer, a German artist and male model. Nicolai himself could have easily been straight out of an Abercrombie and Fitch catalogue for the silver fox generation. He was gorgeous, and most of the students had a crush on him. He and Temple had clicked the day he had arrived seven years ago when she was still a student, and their friendship was the most important thing in Temple's life, apart from Luc. With no other blood relatives, Nicolai *was* her family.

"Listen," he said now, nodding across the room to the dean's table. "Check out the hottie. I hear he's our speaker tomorrow."

Temple looked over to where he was pointing, and for a second, she felt her heart skip a beat. The dean was talking to a man in his late thirties, she guessed, who had the saddest eyes but was also the most beautiful man she had ever seen. His bright green eyes stood out against his dark olive skin and his dark hair. "That's Attico Fibonacci?"

"The one. Didn't expect him to be quite as delicious. Wonder which team he bats for?"

"Ha," Temple grinned. "He's *way* too beautiful to be straight."

Nicolai laughed loudly, which caused several people, including Fibonacci to glance over to their table. Temple's breath caught in her throat as Fibonacci met her gaze ... and held it. Temple felt that glance throughout her body. He didn't look away and neither could she. Temple became aware that the people around her were starting to murmur ... they too could feel the connection crackling in the air between her and this man.

It was too much. She pushed away her chair, breaking the connection, and walked quickly from the room. Nicolai caught up with her, his expression full of concern. "Hey, hey, are you all right? *Ça va?*"

"*Oui, ça va.* I'm okay." She shivered a little. "Walk me to my car, would you?"

"Of course." Nicolai still looked worried, but he walked with her to the parking lot. It was raining, not unusual here, and Temple apologized to him.

Nicolai shook his head. "It's doesn't matter, but tell me, little one ... do you know Fibonacci? Is that why you're upset?"

Temple shook her head. "No, I never met the man ... I'm sorry, just something freaked me out."

"What?"

She gave a half laugh, half sob. "I don't know. Forgive me, Nic. My head's a mess."

He hugged her. "Go home, get some sleep. And don't let Fibonacci get in your head. He's just a rich guy who thinks he can have every woman he sees."

Temple smiled gratefully at him. "Night, Nic."

"Night, Tem."

She drove home and locked the door behind her. She made herself some tea and sat on the window sill. Despite what she told Nic, it didn't take her any time to figure out why Attico Fibonacci's scrutiny had made her so uncomfortable.

A year ago. A night, rainy, like this one. Leaving a bar in Geneva after a night out with her colleagues. A handsome guy who had been making eyes at her all night. She had turned him down, politely.

He had been waiting for her outside.

She'd only just managed to fight him off before someone heard her screams and came to help. The police had been sympathetic but told her they couldn't locate her attacker. Temple had gone home and tried to reason with herself. She hadn't been raped. There was that at least. The one thing she had control over was the one thing that remained intact.

Her virginity. At twenty-eight, she kept it a secret, knowing people would be shocked. She knew people considered her beautiful although she herself could not see it. When she looked in the mirror, she could only see dark brown hair, dark brown eyes, and café au lait skin inherited from her Creole mother and her African-American father. She looked like her mom, soft, rounded. Her mom had been a noted beauty, but she had taught Temple that looks did not matter. Losing her when Temple was five, in a car wreck which had killed her father and her older sister, had been the worst day of her life until Luc's accident. That was when she had known she was truly alone.

So, tonight, as that beautiful man gazed at her, Temple felt a shift in her soul—and her body. It was as if she knew him, her body *knew* him and craved his touch. She shook her head now, feeling stupid. For the love of God, what could you tell from a look? Of all things, Temple did not believe in love at first sight, or even lust at first sight.

But the way her nipples had hardened and her sex had flooded with damp arousal ... "Stop it. Stop it now."

She thought it through logically. Fibonacci was only here for a day to give the commencement speech. She wouldn't even speak to him, despite the fact she had to be at the speech. The dean would command his beloved alumni's attention, she had no doubt.

She sighed with relief. It was paranoia, she thought, that's all. But when she went to bed that night, she couldn't help thinking about his startling green eyes and his beautiful face and knew Attico Fibonacci would haunt her dreams long after he left Geneva.

CHAPTER THREE

Tony knocked on Attico's door just after 9:00 a.m. the next day. Attico, half-shaved, let him in and Tony rolled his eyes. "Late again."

"We have four hours, Tony. Come in, I'm just shaving."

"Obviously." Tony walked into Attico's hotel room and looked around. "Huh. So, the blonde left already?"

"What blonde?"

"The cute blonde who was hitting on you in the bar last night." Tony made a face. "Atti, please tell me you got laid last night?"

Attico didn't answer his brother. They had been out late in one of Geneva's popular nightclubs, but all Attico had wanted to do was drink and then sleep. He still had a hangover now and squinted bloodshot eyes at his brother. "How do you look so good? You had more alcohol than I did."

"I've built up a tolerance, as could you, should you ever decide to lighten up." Tony sighed, brushing down his spotless suit pants. "What about that pretty teacher you had your eye on at the Academy? Did you find out who she was?"

"I didn't ask." Attico said shortly, and returned to the bathroom to finish shaving. He decided against taking his entire beard off but neatened it up. He liked the way it made him look less boyish, like he was someone that should be taken seriously, even if he himself didn't feel like he should.

"Jesus, Atti. Anyone would think you're in your eighties, not your forties."

"*Almost* forty, and at least I'm not acting like a teenager, Tony."

He heard Tony snicker and rolled his eyes. Tony could never take anything seriously. "How about you? Were you entertained last night?"

"Yes, thanks. They were both sweethearts and very discreet. Left early."

Attico sighed and wiped his damp face on a towel. The truth was that, last night, at dinner with the dean of the Academy, he'd been floored by how his body reacted to the young woman sitting at the table across the room. It had been a shock to his system to find himself aroused by her—she was so totally the opposite of Lucinda in every way, to look at, at least. Whereas Lucinda had a willowy, model-sized body, tall, with light blonde hair cut short, and was immaculately made-up, the women—the girl? She barely looked older than the students—was dressed casually in jeans and a faded pink T-shirt, her long dark hair mussed up and loose about her shoulders.

Her face ... God, her face was *exquisite*, and it was all Attico could do not to turn to the dean and ask who she was. Instead, he asked about the woman's neighbor. "I'm sure I recognize him."

"Nicolai Lamont," Dean Corke told him. "Professor of languages. He used to teach at Columbia and I know you've been attached to that school too, with your work with the younger people ... perhaps your paths crossed then?"

"That must be it," Attico lied smoothly, and was disap-

Chapter Three

pointed that the dean didn't take the hint and tell him who the beautiful woman was. They heard Lamont laugh loudly and Attico looked over to her table—and met her gaze. He held it, reading the myriad emotions in her lovely eyes, then started slightly as she pushed back her chair suddenly and left the room.

Everything in his body told her to run after her, but without causing a scene, it was impossible. And he hadn't wanted to frighten her; she was obviously upset about something and he was a stranger. He saw Nicolai Lamont go after her and felt a pang of jealousy. *Stupid. You don't even know her; you've no right to get jealous.*

But he couldn't get her out of his head and after drinking himself into a stupor last night, he'd caught a cab back to his hotel and had fallen asleep in front of the TV.

His head pounded with pain, so he threw back a couple of aspirin before following Tony out of the door. The ceremony was due to start at noon but Dean Corke had asked them to come meet some of the top students in the classes, including the valedictorian.

As the town car made its way around Lake Geneva to the Academy, Attico pulled a wad of papers from his pocket.

"That your speech?"

"Yup." Attico let out a long breath. "It's hokey and cheesy and nothing they haven't heard a million times before. The world is your oyster and all that crap."

"That's what they expect. If you turned up and recited the lyrics to "Baby Got Back," they'd object, I'm sure."

Attico's lips twitched. "Don't tempt me."

Tony grinned. "I'll pay you a million dollars to slip a lyric in."

"You're on."

Tony laughed. "That's more like it."

"Like what?"

"You. Man, I don't want to pile on but the last couple of months, you've been on a downer, which is understandable, but Dad and I were worried."

Attico sighed. "You talked to Dad?"

"Atti ... we still worry every time you get down some."

Attico shook his head but said nothing. He felt guilty, still, even after all these years about his breakdown, that terrible, *terrible* time back in his late teens when depression had consumed him. Despite this, it irritated him when Tony made more of the situation than he needed to. "Tony, anyone would be down after a breakup. Don't make a big deal out of it."

Tony was quiet, then nudged him. "Hey, is Lu still single?"

Attico gaped at him, then realized Tony was kidding. "Douchebag."

"Pussy."

Attico chuckled, his mood lightening. When they got to the Academy, Dean Corke came to greet them personally. "I hope you enjoyed Geneva's nightlife, gentlemen."

Tony and Attico exchanged a look and grinned. "Certainly."

Dean Corke took them through the day's schedule. "A drinks reception at 11:00 a.m. with the valedictorian and some of the staff, then at noon the ceremony. We'll have robes for you to wear, Mr. Fibonacci," he said to Attico, who smiled as Tony snickered.

"Fine."

The dean led them through the ancient halls of the school. Really, it was a beautiful building, all stone and sculpture. "Hogwarts," Tony had said yesterday as they had arrived. "I forgot we went to Hogwarts."

Attico was reminded of that now and so he was still smiling as the dean led him into the staffroom, a large, dark-wood paneled room with priceless artwork and an elaborate chandelier. Money was not a problem for this school.

Some of the teachers were introduced to him and Tony chatted easily—well, he made it *look* easy, anyway—to them as the drinks circulated. They were introduced to the valedictorian, a young African-American woman named Zella who shook their hands seriously but had a twinkle in her eyes. "So, if you're both alumni, you know all the secrets of the school? All the gossip?"

Dean Corke chuckled and Attico smiled a little uncomfortably.

"Not much to tell," Tony said smoothly, and Attico was grateful for the save. Dean Corke shot him a glance and Attico knew he, too, was relieved that Tony had brushed the question aside.

Twenty minutes later and Attico snuck a look at his watch. He was just contemplating a bathroom break, just to escape the throng of people, when he saw her.

Her dark hair was swept up into a messy bun at the nape of her neck, her curvaceous body poured into a dark burgundy dress which clung to the outline of her full breasts. A simple gold chain was around her neck and there was the barest minimum of makeup on her sweet face. As Attico watched, she skirted the edge of the party and headed for the drinks table. Shooting a look at the dean and Tony, who were deep in conversation, Attico moved quietly to her side.

"Hello," he said softly, and saw her start a little before she turned to him. Up close, he saw her eyes were a deep chocolate brown, there was a faint flush of pink on her cheeks, and her mouth was full, beautifully shaped, and a delicate shade of pink.

"Hello." Her voice was breathy and low, but without the annoying vocal fry so many women of his acquaintance used nowadays. Her large eyes studied him and Attico felt as if she were assessing him. He held out his hand.

"Attico Fibonacci."

She looked at his hand for a moment before shaking it—and he was sure she felt the same jolt as he did when his skin touched hers. "Temple Dubois."

Temple ... it suited her. "I'm speaking at commencement," he prompted when it became clear he would have to lead the conversation. "Do you teach here?"

"Sorry, sorry," she said, shaking herself and giving a nervous laugh. "I teach some of the history classes, mostly concentrating on artifacts. A geek," she said, with a sudden smile and he chuckled.

"Geeks are the best."

"You're an alumnus, I hear."

Attico nodded. "I am. Actually, it's exactly twenty years since I graduated this year."

Temple Dubois nodded, but he saw a wariness creep into her eyes—did she know the history of what had happened here back then? "Did you know Luc Monfils?"

Oh fuck. Don't lie. "I did. Terrible, what happened to him."

She nodded and looked away. "I came to live here shortly after that."

Attico was confused by the seeming change of subject. "You must have been very young to come here."

Temple shook her head. "It doesn't matter. Listen, I see Dean Corke heading over here, no doubt to collect you for your speech. Good luck with it."

"Thank you. It was good to meet you, Mademoiselle Dubois."

Temple smiled at him and his stomach constricted with desire. "Temple, please, and the same to you. Mr. Fibonacci."

He would have told her to call him Attico, but she was gone too quickly, and he felt bereft. God, she was beautiful, and there was something so vulnerable about her that made him want to wrap his arms around her and protect her from the world. He wanted to know more, but then Dean Corke hurried him away to get robed up and Attico had to push all thoughts of Temple Dubois to one side.

Temple herself had had to escape from Attico Fibonacci's company because she couldn't cope with the sensations his presence was sending throughout her body. Her skin felt aflame, her heart beat too fast, and a throbbing pulse beat between her legs. What the hell? She had never felt like that in a man's presence before and it made her a little panicky. It couldn't be a good thing, surely?

The man was a stranger, and now she knew—he had known Luc. He had been here when Luc had his accident. When the girl had been murdered. Attico Fibonacci had known her brother. It seemed fate that they'd met now, but did it follow that it was a good thing?

She was saved from dwelling on that fact as the commencement ceremony began and her students trooped up onto the stage to receive their degrees and their congratulations. Zella gave a rousing speech to her fellow students and friends, making Temple proud, and then it was Fibonacci's turn to talk.

Temple took the opportunity to study him. There was no doubt, she thought, that Attico Fibonacci was a sensational looking man, Hollywood superstar-looks, and he had a presence about him, something undefinable.

She felt a nudge and looked up to see Nicolai grinning at her as he sat down next to her. "Still eyeing the Fabulous Fibonacci? I have to admit, he's a looker."

Temple felt her face burn and Nicolai noticed, his grin widening. "You like him."

"I don't know him."

"Is he tingling your biscuits?"

Temple shoved her elbow into his side. "Shh, I'm trying to listen."

She watched Attico as he gave his speech, which, while not earth-shattering and Kennedy-like, was interesting enough that she saw her students nodding along. As he drew to the end, she saw a twinkle come into his eye, a little mischief in his expression. "As for your future, I cannot lie, there will be chances and opportunities, but with them will come big 'buts.' An opportunity will arise, but you may have to take a drop in salary to do it or move somewhere away from your family. There will always be big 'buts' in every decision you make, I can't deny."

Temple half grinned. She saw Fibonacci's brother smothering a chuckle behind his hand and got it. She started to laugh quietly, and as she did, Attico looked over at her and smiled. God, cute, sexy, and *funny*. Damn it, he really was the full package, wasn't he?

She was still smiling when she made her way down to the students who, released from the formality of the occasion, were chatting excitedly about the party later on.

Zella hugged Temple. "You are coming, right?"

"I am, of course, I want to be there for you all. God, I'm so proud of you all," Temple said to the small group of students with her. Barry, the blond quarterback-like sweetheart, grinned at her.

"Now that you're no longer our official tutor, can we admit our crushes on you?"

Temple rolled her eyes, chuckling. "Absolutely not, and don't forget, this summer school won't be a cakewalk. You want it on your transcripts, I'll make you work for it."

"Zel says you won't give anything away about the exhibit."

"Good." The voice came from behind her and Temple's

colleague and deputy-dean, Brett Forrester appeared. The students murmured a greeting respectfully, and Temple nodded at Brett.

He smiled at her. "Temple, might have I have a moment of your time?"

"Of course, Deputy-Dean Forrester."

She winked at her students and followed Forrester out of the room. He was one of the few people who had been here longer than Temple, a man in his late forties who had gone from valedictorian to tutor to deputy dean. The rest of the staff were wary of his unhidden ambition, and even Dean Corke spoke to him with deference.

Temple was wary of him for a different reason. Brett Forrester was an attractive man, and he knew it, and he'd made overtures to her in the past, but Temple had always politely turned him down. "We work together, Brett," she'd said evenly. "And one of my rules is not to get involved with colleagues."

Now, though, she felt her heart sink. Brett smiled at her. "As you know, Temple, this semester is my last here at the Academy, but I will still be involved in the summer school."

"I didn't know that." *Damn it.*

Brett nodded. "Oh yes. The curator of the museum is a good friend of mine, and he asked me if I could oversee the loan of the artefacts."

Temple felt the sting. "He doesn't trust me?"

Brett gave a short laugh, putting his hand against the wall, leaning toward her. Temple backed off against the stone. "Don't worry, sweet Temple, there're no issues there. I just told him how close we were and that I'd be sitting in on some of the classes. That's all."

Nope. No. Not going to happen. "Brett, this class is very important to me, and to my students. There cannot be any distractions."

Brett smiled and leaned closer. "I look forward to working closely with you."

Ugh, slime ball. She pushed away from him, irked and pissed, but he grabbed her hand. "Come on, Temple. We both know this has been in the cards between us for years."

"What's been in the cards, Brett? You refusing to take no for an answer?" Temple had had enough now and Brett's face flashed with anger.

"You superior little whore. You've always thought yourself better than me."

Temple opened her mouth to reply, but then, out of the shadows at the end of the dark hallway, Attico Fibonacci stepped into the light. His brooding eyes were fixed on Brett, and Temple gave an involuntary shiver. Attico looked dangerous, more dangerous than she'd ever seen any man look. Dangerous and devastatingly sexy.

"*Bonsoir,*" he said evenly. "Mademoiselle Dubois, *ça va?*" His eyes dared Brett to answer for her.

"I'm fine, thank you, Mr. Fibonacci." Temple let the gratitude she felt make itself clear in her tone. Attico walked towards them. Brett, not wanting to give ground, edged closer to Temple, but Attico offered his arm to Temple, still looking at Brett.

"Shall we? I have reservations at Il Lago."

Temple didn't hesitate and took his arm. "I'm looking forward to it, thank you. Good night, Brett."

She wanted to laugh at the expression on his face. Brett wasn't anywhere near the same league as Attico Fibonacci and he knew it. Temple walked with Attico out to the front of the school, then turned to him. "Thank you, Mr. Fibonacci. I appreciate the rescue."

Attico grinned at her. "I thought you might. Brett Forrester is a sleaze."

"He is, and you probably saved me from an arrest too. He

was about to get punched in the face." She gave a half-shocked laugh at her own words. "Not that I'm a violent person."

"Forrester could drive a person to it. I doubt anyone would blame you." He smiled at her. "And the invitation to dinner stands. I *do* have reservations at Il Lago. I'd be delighted if you would join me, but absolutely no pressure or obligation."

Temple gazed up at him. Every cell in her body was screaming at her to accept and she nodded. "I would like that."

Attico, to her surprise, looked relieved. *Really?* A man like him was nervous of asking *her* out? Come on ... this had to be an act ... didn't it?

"I'm very happy to hear that. I was driven here so I need to call a cab ..."

"Well, if you don't mind being driven by a woman in an ancient Volkswagen, my car is in the parking lot." She smiled back at him as he laughed. He was fun, certainly, and Temple found herself excited about spending more time with him.

"Lead on." He offered her his arm again—such a gentleman—and they walked to the parking lot. He chuckled when he saw her car. The pale blue Volkswagen Beetle was held together with rust and duct tape but Temple loved it. She grinned when she saw his amusement.

"I like big bugs and I cannot lie," she said to him, her tongue firmly in her cheek, and he laughed.

"Touché."

They got in as Temple shoved a handful of books from the passenger seat into the back. "Sorry, it's always an absolute pit."

"No, I like it."

"Also, the heating doesn't work."

"Always helpful in the Alps," Attico laughed, and she grinned.

"Sorry." She started the car, wincing when it gave a groan.

Attico chuckled. "Sure it's going to make it into the city?"

"Oh ye of little faith." She turned to him. "Sure you don't have to tell anyone you're leaving? Your brother? The dean?"

Attico smiled. "I'm my own man. I've done what they asked of me. Now I get to enjoy myself."

Temple let the car idle while she studied him. "Mr. Fibonacci ..."

"Attico."

"Attico ... me agreeing to dinner is just that. *Dinner*. So, if you're expecting anything else ..."

He held up his hands. "I'm just grateful you agreed to dinner, Temple. I'm not expecting anything."

Temple felt relief—and not a little disappointment at his words. He was glorious, but if he thought she would leap straight into bed with him, he had another thing coming ...

however tempting that prospect might be.

Temple drove into the city, and he directed her to the hotel. Il Lago was at the Four Seasons Hotel and Temple's eyes widened as Attico led her inside. "I think I'm underdressed."

It was Attico's opinion that she was far too *over*dressed for his liking but he kept that to himself. He sensed Temple would not be comfortable if he told her honestly what her presence, her company, the scent of her skin was doing to his body. That her clean, fresh perfume was driving him crazy, that the heat of her hand on his arm made him want to pull her into the darkest alcove here and kiss her until they were both breathless.

Instead he pulled out her chair for her, smiled as she thanked him, and sat down opposite her. "Well, this is a very unexpected pleasure," he said and chuckled. "I promise you, I don't often do this."

Temple looked at him skeptically and he held up his hands. "It's true, despite what the papers might say. I was in a long-term relationship for years and since that ended, I've not been on a date."

"Who said this was a date?" But she was grinning, and he chuckled.

"Touché. *Again*."

"Did you enjoy today?" Temple thanked him as he handed her a menu and nodded when he asked her if red wine was okay.

"I'm not a huge fan of public speaking, but it was ..." He thought for a second. "It was interesting to be back here again."

"You haven't returned since your own graduation." Temple colored a little. "I would have remembered."

Attico held her gaze. "Now I wish I had."

They stared at each other for a long moment, then Attico grinned and Temple laughed. "It's going to be one of those conversations, isn't it? Double meanings in everything we say ..."

"... and awkward flirting from me," Attico said ruefully.

"You, awkward? I can't see that." Temple smiled at him. "No one that looks like you could ever be awkward."

"I may just surprise you, Temple Dubois. Tell me ... how come you've lived at the school for so long?"

Temple hesitated, and he was sad to see wariness creep into her eyes. "My family ... I was alone, suddenly, when I was eight. The school—" She trailed off and shook her head as if arguing with herself. "The school bore some responsibility for that. I had been living here with my older brother—"

Suddenly Attico got it. With a sinking heart, he closed his eyes and nodded. "Luc."

"Yes. Luc is my brother. As you know, he was accused of murdering a young woman, amongst other things, and he tried to commit suicide."

Attico's heart was pounding. "I know. God, Temple, I'm so sorry. Luc was ..."

Temple gave a rueful smile. "Can't quite say 'innocent, can you? It's okay, the evidence was pretty damning."

A cloud had settled over their table and Attico risked touching the back of her hand lightly. "I am sorry, Temple, I really am."

"There's been a lot of rumors over the years but no one who seems to know what the hell was going on back then."

"What kind of rumors?" Attico felt dismay in his heart that this lovely young woman had had to live with this horror all these years.

"About a secret society Luc was involved in ... Look, sorry, it's not exactly cheerful dinner conversation, I'm sorry. Let's change the subject."

She smiled at him, but Attico knew then he could not pursue any sort of relationship with her. He knew too much ... he had *done* too much ... and this was his penance.

Goddamn it ...

Temple noticed the change in Attico's mood and wondered if she had done the right thing by telling him so much. He had been there—maybe reminding him of what happened had been the wrong thing, but she had a hard time lying to someone who had been there, someone who could tell her what it was like ...

But she felt tearful now as the atmosphere between them changed. The dinner was excellent, and they chatted easily still, but the heat that had been there was gone. Attico offered to escort her home, but she politely declined. "Thank you for dinner, Attico."

He kissed her cheek, leaving her skin burning. "It was an honor to meet you, Temple."

And he was gone. Temple sighed and started her car, driving home, then clumping despondently up her stairs to her apartment.

"Dammit," she said, throwing her purse on the couch. She felt so deflated. "Why did you get so heavy? You scared him away!"

But the need to have her questions answered by someone who had been there when Luc ...

No. She pushed the thought away. Attico Fibonacci had been a pleasant diversion for an evening, but that was it. He was neither the answer to her questions, nor a potential lover. *First lover.* Temple groaned and buried her face in a pillow. She knew now what it felt like to be so turned on by someone that her body felt like it was crying out for his touch. She clutched the pillow tightly and let herself imagine what it would have been like to make love to Attico.

Those eyes, that heavy, brooding brow of his sending shivers up and down her body as he approached, those long, well-manicured fingers on her body, sliding her dress from her shoulders. His strong legs, the broad shoulders, that mouth, that sensual mouth on her own, then on her body, moving down ...

"Stop it!" she growled into the pillow, then threw it across the room. *Stop acting like a child.* Attico Fibonacci wasn't just out of her league, he was in a whole different solar system, and the fact that she had told him she wasn't going to sleep with him just because he bought her dinner ... well, he'd lost all interest, clearly.

Sighing, Temple got up and went to her bedroom, stripping off before going to take a shower. Later, in bed, she read for a while before falling asleep and dreaming of being naked with Attico and giving up all of her inhibitions as he made sweet love to her ...

CHAPTER FOUR

Attico thanked the driver as he stepped out of the town car into the airport. Tony was ahead of him, all ready to board their private jet, but Attico felt almost bereft. He hadn't looked forward to coming here in the first place but now it felt like he had unfinished business.

Temple Dubois. He couldn't get her out of his head, both because he was attracted to her physically, and also because he was someone who had known her brother, Luc, before his accident. He, Attico, could help her find the answers she was looking for ... but it would cost him. It would cost him a lot.

"Hey, douchebag, you ready?"

Sometimes it was easy to forget that Tony was a fifty-five-year-old man. Attico gave him the finger and smiled. "Just reminiscing."

"About the hot teacher? Yeah, I know you hooked up with her last night."

"We had dinner, and that's all."

Tony rolled his eyes. "It was on a silver platter and you didn't go for it?"

Attico felt irked at Tony's disrespect for Temple. "Mademoiselle Dubois is a class act, Tony. I'm not surprised you didn't recognize it."

"Oo, bitch." Tony was amused, but when he saw Attico wasn't smiling, he relented. "You like her, huh?"

Attico nodded. "But there's no future there."

Tony waited until they were on the jet before he spoke again. "Why, Atti? You've not looked at another woman since Lucinda, and now that you've met this teacher girl—"

"Her brother is Luc Monfils."

Understanding crossed Tony's face. "Ah."

"So, you can see why I'm not pursuing this."

Tony half smiled. "Even though you like her."

"She's beautiful, smart, funny … and I helped destroy her life."

"Atti."

Attico shook his head. "Don't. Just don't."

Tony sighed but stay silent. Attico stared out of the window as the jet moved down the runway, getting into position for lift off. Temple Dubois had been a sweet diversion but there was no way he could stay and see if their attraction led to anything.

No way.

The week Temple spent reading and chilling out had been welcomed but now she was ready to teach her classes for the summer. It helped, too, that preparing her lessons had distracted her from the fact that she hadn't heard from Attico Fibonacci after that one night. She had to admit—it hurt a little, but, she reasoned, some people just drop into your life for a brief moment and change your outlook.

And he had. Just for the one night, he had made her feel interesting, beautiful, feminine. Desirable. *A gorgeous man wanted me*, she said to herself and smiled. Even if nothing had come of it, it was still a good feeling.

Now, as she made her way to her lecture theater, she was smiling and didn't see Brett Forrester appear beside her until he spoke. "Did you enjoy your date with Fibonacci?"

Temple sighed. "That's none of your business, Brett."

He smiled thinly. "You know, I might be leaving the school after the summer, but I still have some sway with the dean. You might want to be nicer to me."

"I don't respond to threats, Deputy-Dean," Temple said, her voice clear and loud so that the students could hear her, and Brett backed off with a supercilious smile. He sat down at the back of the class and Temple sighed. *Just ignore him.*

She smiled at her students. "Hey all, thanks for enrolling in this class. Obviously, it's outside the normal curriculum, but it will be a credit that you can show on your academic transcripts."

Temple perched on the edge of her desk. "So, as you all know, the Museum D'Nuit has loaned the school some of its more controversial artefacts for an exhibition here in a couple of weeks. The art faculty has very kindly allowed us access to the artifacts before they go on show, so you'll get up close, physical access."

She grinned at her students. "Now I know some of the more curious—or nosy—of you have already been guessing as to which items we're getting and yes, now I can confirm we will be getting a close look at *Le Tarot Du Sang D'Hiver*—the Tarot of Winter Blood."

A small rumble of appreciation went through the class and Temple chuckled. "Now, for those of you who don't know, the tarot deck is one of the oldest ever discovered, and it was discovered right here, at the Academy, during building work around twenty-two years ago."

She turned to her laptop and cued up an image of a tarot card. It depicted a woman blindfolded and tied to a stake with a demonic figure dancing around her. "This is one of the few cards which doesn't show actual violence. As you know, the deck is controversial for its depictions of graphic violence and is considered one of the most misogynistic decks ever produced. For that reason, the school gave it away to the museum, where it has been the subject of protests and controversy, for obvious reasons."

One of her students put his hand up. "Yes, Damon?"

Damon, a jock from New England money, smiled. "Will we get to see the whole deck? Even the Major Arcana?"

"Of course. The dean has given his permission and, as you are all over eighteen, we didn't need permission from your parents, although I certainly hope you discussed this with them. I know some people had concerns over the occult nature of some of these artifacts, but as we made clear, this isn't a class which deals with beliefs. This is purely art history."

Temple ran through some of the other items they'd be studying for the rest of the class and set up a schedule for them to visit the exhibition. "Obviously, usual rules apply, no cell phones, cameras, gum, or liquids near the pieces, please."

"The school expects you all to be on your best behavior," Brett Forrester spoke up from the back of the room, prompting eye rolls from most of the class.

"Well, as we're all adults here …" Temple said, flint in her voice as she glared at him.

"Temple?" Rosario de Silva raised her hand and Temple smiled at her.

"Yes, hon?"

"Is it true that the deck was linked to a murder back in the day?"

Temple felt her chest tighten. She'd been expecting the question. "That's something we'll be discussing when we actually see the pieces. Okay, for now, class dismissed. Thanks everyone."

She made her way back to her office, avoiding an approaching Brett, and shutting the door behind her. Her eyes widened when she saw the flowers on her desk. Who ...?

Somehow, as she opened the card, she knew.

I can't stop thinking about you, Temple Dubois.
Attico Fibonacci.

In the envelope, too, was another small card—an invitation to an art exhibition in Paris at the weekend.

Say yes and I'll send the jet to pick you up. Say yes, Temple.

Temple felt her face burn and her stomach curl with pleasure and surprise. *Wow.* The thought of seeing him again made her body ache, yearn, even though in reality, he was still a stranger to her.

His cell phone number was on the card and before she could talk herself out of it, she called him. He answered on the first ring. "Hello, Temple."

"Yes," she said, almost breathless. "Yes, I will come to Paris."

"Good," Attico said, and again she sensed his relief. "I can't wait to see you again."

"Just so you know ..."

"I'm not expecting anything but your company, sweetheart, I swear." God, his deep voice made her belly squirm with desire.

"So we're clear."

He chuckled. "We are. I just wanted to see you again."

"Paris."

"I can't wait. See you at the weekend."

CHAPTER FIVE

New York...

Attico ended the call with the biggest smile on his face. It had been a week since he had seen her and it was too long. He hadn't talked about it with Tony, but this morning, on impulse he'd had the idea. A friend of his, Maceo Bartoli, was holding an exhibition in Paris at his new gallery, and seeing the invitation on his desk, Attico had known he wanted to invite Temple.

Now she had agreed, and he called his assistant, Jeph, in to arrange the private jet. Jeph, a slinky hipster from Queens, grinned at him. "Gossip?"

Attico rolled his eyes. He and Jeph had worked together for so long now that they were almost family and Attico was always amused at Jeph's penchant for gossiping.

"Met a cute girl in Switzerland."

Jeph's eyes lit up. "Goody. Tell me more."

"Not much to tell yet, except she's agreed to fly to Paris to meet me this weekend. Can you send the jet?"

He gave Jeph all the details and his assistant got up to leave the room. "Oh wait." He turned back to Attico, and this time he wasn't smiling. "I saw Lucinda at George the other night."

Attico sighed. What now? Jeph seemed hesitant. "Atti ... she's pregnant."

Ouch. Like a brick bat to the chest. "Well ... I hope she's happy," he said evenly, nodding at Jeph. Jeph read the signal to leave Attico alone and closed the door quietly behind him.

Attico turned his chair to look out over Manhattan. *Pregnant.* How many years had they tried and not been successful and now, within months, she was pregnant?

"Fuck." He said it quietly, but the pain was real. He longed for a child—something he hadn't confided to anyone, *ever*. Every month he had been with Lucinda, he'd been so excited for her to say that she was late, that she had taken a test and that they were going to be parents. He was almost forty—he wanted kids soon so that he was still fit and able enough to play and run with them.

He glanced at the clock. He had a late meeting with some clients tonight, but until then ... he grabbed his bag and headed out. He drove to his gym and worked out, getting all the frustration he felt out. On the treadmill, he stuck his earbuds into his ears and turned the music up as he ran for miles.

After a half hour, he slowed his pace, noticing that there was only one other person using the facilities, a middle-aged man whom he'd only recently seen using the facilities. Attico nodded politely.

"Hey there." The man was puffing on the adjacent treadmill and Attico had the strange idea that he'd been trying to keep pace with him.

"Hey." Attico wiped his face and stepped off the treadmill. It wasn't usual for the gym's clientele to start conversations and so he was surprised when the man slowed his own pace and smiled at him.

"Denny Fleet." He stuck his hand out and, not wanting to be rude, Attico shook it.

"Attico Fibonacci."

"Oh, I know. You're famous around here. The new building on Fifth is spectacular."

Attico gave him a polite smile. "Thank you, but it's really down to the architects on my team."

"Ah, don't put yourself down. I've seen your other work, here, Seattle, Chicago. Big fan."

"You follow property?"

Denny nodded. "I do. Frustrated architect. Family wanted me to go into banking, always regretted it."

"Never too late to change."

"Ah, I don't know. Anyway, good to meet you."

"You too."

Attico finished his workout and headed for the showers. As he left the gym parking lot a while later, he didn't see the car following him, nor when it parked outside his offices. The driver watched him as Attico went inside, then silently pulled away and drove off into the night.

If you want to continue reading this story, you can get your copy from your favorite vendor by searching for the title:

Her Dark Secret
A Billionaire & A Virgin Romance

You can also find the e-book version by typing this link in your computer's browser:

https://www.hotandsteamyromance.com/products/her-dark-secret-a-billionaire-a-virgin-romance

OTHER BOOKS BY THIS AUTHOR

Saving Her Rescuer: A Billionaire & A Virgin Romance

I WAS JUST TRYING to get away from my crazy ex for the weekend when I ended up in a giant pileup on the highway up to Gore Mountain.

HTTPS://GENI.US/SAVINGHERRESCUER

~

SENSUAL SOUNDS: A Rockstar Ménage

LUST. Lies. Double lives.

The rock and roll industry is full of people who are looking out for themselves and willing to do anything to rise to the top.

https://www.hotandsteamyromance.com/collections/frontpage/products/sensual-sounds-a-rockstar-menage

∾

On the Run: A Secret Baby Romance

Murder. Lies. Fraud. Just another day in the lives of billionaires and women on the run.

https://www.hotandsteamyromance.com/collections/frontpage/products/on-the-run-a-secret-baby-romance

∾

The Dirty Doctor's Touch: A Billionaire Doctor Romance

I am a master. An elitist. I am at the top of my field, and I know what I am doing.

https://www.hotandsteamyromance.com/collections/frontpage/products/the-dirty-doctor-s-touch-a-billionaire-doctor-romance

The Hero She Needs: A Single Daddy Next Door Romance

He's the only man I've ever wanted...

https://www.hotandsteamyromance.com/collections/frontpage/products/the-hero-she-needs-a-single-daddy-next-door-romance

You can find all of my books here

Hot and Steamy Romance
https://www.hotandsteamyromance.com

ABOUT THE AUTHOR

Mrs. Love writes about smart, sexy women and the hot alpha billionaires who love them. She has found her own happily ever after with her dream husband and adorable 6 and 2 year old kids.

Currently, Michelle is hard at work on the next book in the series, and trying to stay off the Internet.

"Thank you for supporting an indie author. Anything you can do, whether it be writing a review, or even simply telling a fellow reader that you enjoyed this. Thanks

 facebook.com/HotAndSteamyRomance
 instagram.com/michellesromance

COPYRIGHT

©Copyright 2020 by Michelle Love, All rights Reserved

In no way is it legal to reproduce, duplicate, or transmit any part of this document in either electronic means or in printed format. Recording of this publication is strictly prohibited and any storage of this document is not allowed unless with written permission from the publisher. All rights are reserved. Respective authors own all copyrights not held by the publisher.

www.ingramcontent.com/pod-product-compliance
Lightning Source LLC
LaVergne TN
LVHW011711060526
838200LV00051B/2864